'Ha⋯
New Y⋯

'A vivid journey into w⋯
and the bonds of family'
Booklist

'*The Blue Maiden* is a shimmering spell of a novel:
mesmerizing, beautiful, and alive with pain, wonder, rage
and love. Simply stunning'
Emma Törzs, author of *Ink Blood Sister Scribe*

'It is partly a young girl's coming of age in the mid-nineteenth
century, and partly a treatise of the wildness in women. *The Blue
Maiden* haunted me long after I put it down'
Stephanie Danler, author of *Sweetbitter*

'This perfect book stands all on its own. Terrifying, but real.
I loved it so much'
Jenny Slate, author of *Little Weirds*

'*The Blue Maiden* is a knockout by a writer at the height
of her exquisite powers'
Julie Buntin, author of *Marlena*

'Every sentence is resplendent, assured; every scene
gripping and intimate. An exquisite homage to sisterhood,
a treasure, a masterpiece'
Claire Luchette, author of *Agatha of Little Neon*

'A spectacular novel of sisterly devotion and the sacred bonds
formed of loss and secrecy. What a gift Noyes has bequeathed to us'
Chịkọdịlị Emelụmadụ, author of *Dazzling*

Also by Anna Noyes

Goodnight, Beautiful Women

About the Author

Anna Noyes' debut collection, *Goodnight, Beautiful Women*, was a finalist for the Story Prize and the New England Book Award, as well as a *New York Times* Editors' Choice, Indie Next Pick, Barnes and Noble Discover Great New Writers Selection, and Amazon Best Book of the Month. She holds an MFA from the Iowa Writers' Workshop. Her fiction has appeared in *Vice*, *A Public Space*, and *Guernica*, among others. She has received the Lotos Foundation Prize and the Henfield Prize, as well as residencies from MacDowell, Yaddo, Lighthouse Works, the James Merrill House, and Aspen Words. She lives in New York, on Fishers Island.

THE
BLUE
MAIDEN

ANNA
NOYES

atlantic · *fiction*

First published in the United States of America in 2024 by Grove Press,
an imprint of Grove Atlantic.

First published in hardback in Great Britain in 2024 by Atlantic Books,
an imprint of Atlantic Books Ltd.

This paperback edition published in 2025

Copyright © Anna Noyes, 2024

The moral right of Anna Noyes to be identified as the author of this
work has been asserted by her in accordance with the Copyright,
Designs and Patents Act of 1988.

All rights reserved. No part of this publication may be reproduced, stored
in a retrieval system, or transmitted in any form or by any means, electronic,
mechanical, photocopying, recording, or otherwise, without the prior
permission of both the copyright owner and the above publisher of this book.

No part of this book may be used in any manner in the learning, training or
development of generative artificial intelligence technologies (including but
not limited to machine learning models and large language models (LLMs)),
whether by data scraping, data mining or use in any way to create or form a
part of data sets or in any other way.

This novel is entirely a work of fiction. The names, characters and incidents
portrayed in it are the work of the author's imagination. Any resemblance to
actual persons, living or dead, events or localities, is entirely coincidental.

1 2 3 4 5 6 7 8 9

A CIP catalogue record for this book is available from the British Library.

Paperback ISBN: 978 1 78649 583 9
EBook ISBN: 978 1 78649 582 2

Printed and bound in Great Britain by Clays Ltd, Elcograf S.p.A.

Atlantic Books
An Imprint of Atlantic Books Ltd
Ormond House
26–27 Boswell Street
London
WC1N 3JZ

www.atlantic-books.co.uk

Product safety EU representative: Authorised Rep Compliance Ltd., Ground Floor,
71 Lower Baggot Street, Dublin, D02 P593, Ireland. www.arccompliance.com

MIX
Paper | Supporting
responsible forestry
FSC® C018072

For Isla

When all the witches in your town have been set on fire, their smoke will fill your mouth. It will teach you new words. It will tell you what you've done.

—ELIZABETH WILLIS

I coupled with dust in the shadow of a stone.
My ankles brighten. Brightness ascends my thighs.
I am lost, I am lost, in the robes of all this light.

—SYLVIA PLATH

Part I

Berggrund Island, Sweden

1675

Today, wash day.

The island's thirty-two women wake before dawn. This is their favorite time, wind not yet alive on the water, as if the wind sleeps also.

Wives turn to the broad, freckled backs of their husbands. The children stare from the doorway then come burrowing in, crowns of their heads burning but their feet unfathomably cold. They smell mossy, of addled sleep, damp sweat. Their sheets will be scoured. The children, lately, suffer nightmares they cannot remember.

Across town, women attend to the morning.

One is greeted by a vole's mauled body, laid out on her doorstep. Another presses damp tea leaves to the fleabites ringing her ankles. A third sips cream off the top of the milk, then puffs on her dead father's pipe. Ash is shoveled, chicken thighs taken from the ice chest and salted. In the dustpan, a curled black shape is mistaken for a snake, but no, only a leek, petrified from hiding many months under the cookstove. The baby inside Signe hiccoughs. Ida watches the ocean from her stoop for the day's first waves, sketching a new drawing in her book. Not a specimen this time but an image from her imagination: a long line of women wading into water.

The priest waits for them at the church gate.

The sky pinks, across the street the grassland cast in soft hues that will harshen by half past six.

Beside him stand the orphan brothers, farmhands seven and eleven years old. The older brother trims their hair crooked with sheep shears. Their vests are flecked with hay because they sleep beside the goats for warmth and comfort.

Last night the priest—knowing they were starving—plied them with a supper of plums, pork loin, and hard-boiled eggs. They ate on haybales. "Let me tell you a story," the priest said. "About the two of you. I have a vision you will help me." But they were not listening, absorbed in sucking their sour plum pits, so he suggested one more treat. He'd catch them two pike and fry them crisp.

The priest knows the village children whisper that his legs are too long for his torso, and his house too tall and thin. When he rides his scrawny horse through town his feet drag the ground, leaving a cloud of dust.

At the stream, hooked pike flapping on the bank, he held the young boy's head under the water. He had explained himself quite carefully over their dinner. He was willing to explain himself once more. "Stop," begged the older one, pounding the priest's back. "I'll confess anything you want. We'll do anything at all."

The priest explained as the water churned how he simply did what God told him to. "God," said the priest, lifting the small boy who gasped and dripped, "might as well be holding my own head underwater."

The church bell tolls.

The orphans do as they've been told, pointing discreetly to the women filing past with their families while the priest notes the chosen in his ledger.

The older boy imagines the spot on the women's foreheads as the whorl of an inked fingerprint. The younger sees something purple and raised, like the birthmark on the butcher's wife's cheek.

"Why pick so many?" the older chides his brother when they're hurried last of all through the doors.

"Because I saw it," he answers too loudly. "The Devil's mark." Already he looks like he could cry.

The priest leads the village in song, limestone walls echoing, even in summer radiating cold. He leads them in prayer. They kneel on cushions the women embroidered as girls, some by chance bending to their own childish handiwork or their mother's needlepoint of wild roses, their grandmother's sea grapes. He waits as their daughters tuck limp bouquets of fern, lily, and bloodroot around the oxidized plaques by the door, honoring the dead.

When he reads from his ledger in the smooth voice of a sermon, the women blush to hear their names issue from his mouth.

He tells them they've been marked.

The youngest is fifteen, the eldest has just celebrated her birthday. "One hundred and two," she insisted to doubting great-great-grandchildren, "and even I was your age once." But they could not believe a person so old could ever have been so young.

As the orphans are called to the pulpit, they hold hands.

"She's who took us," says the little brother, pointing to the butcher's wife in the front pew, purple birthmark curled around her eye. Some days she gifts him scraps of crisp chicken skin, humming as she bustles.

"Where did she take you?" asks the priest.

"To Blockula," answers his brother. "To the Devil waiting there."

The villagers gasp to hear the Blue Maiden called by its dark name. Demon spirits are said to awaken at the sound. The name is archaic. No one remembers the naming: the Devil's home has always been Blockula. It will always be. Innocent villagers cannot find Blockula, for it hides from the uncorrupted eye. Blockula is reached by witch's flight, riding beasts or broomsticks or slumbering men. There you'll find a meadow stretching into endless distance, a circular labyrinth to get lost in forever, and the Devil's house with its door open.

The Blue Maiden, barren of houses and people, shows no sign of its shadow realm. She is the little sister island to Berggrund, domed like a hill rising from the water while Berggrund is low-lying, long, and narrow.

All summer, the priest has preached of mainland women in evil covenant, abducting children and flying them over the water, sacrificing their souls in Satan's midnight meadow. Reports of carnality, unslakable hunger, candles made from the rendered fat of babes. Parish after parish has exacted due punishment.

Until now, no Berggrunder has been accused, though they are nearest to the Blue Maiden, whose stark silhouette is visible from the mainland only on the clearest days. Berggrund's villagers are afraid even to think the name Blockula, but the Blue Maiden's offshore presence is a constant reminder, like a needling speck of soot in the corner of the eye.

The priest clears his throat, and the orphan boy fears there's something he's forgotten. He describes the black-gummed goat the witch flew them on.

"And what else?" the priest asks.

"A meadow," he answers, "that goes on forever. And in it, a gray house. The Devil's house was tall and thin."

"Good," says the priest. "Enough."

He will not make them speak what comes next, visions God has gifted him, terribly, nightly. How within the great room of Blockula's house, Berggrund Island's treacherous women waited on their backs in rows upon rows of slim beds. How the Devil visited them, one by one. He tells this part himself. "Who knows what creatures grow in their wombs now," he says.

Signe cups her rounded belly, the baby fluttering inside.

She can almost remember it: rickety bed, outside the window a meadow without end, the Devil with long fingers opening her legs.

"But first," the priest continues, "they feasted. And what were you fed, at the Devil's table?"

The meal that comes to the older boy's mind was once his mother's favorite.

"Speak up," says the priest.

"Cabbage with bacon," he repeats, heavy with shame.

"And bread and butter," says the younger. "Cheese, milk, and cream, and plum cake."

"And how did it taste?"

"Very good," the young one says. While his brother answers, "Rotten," then corrects himself: "One bite good. The next, spoiled."

"Tell me,"—the priest opens wide his arms to the congregation—"are such simple boys capable of such elaborate lies?"

"I dined there, too," shouts the candlemaker's daughter, Ursa, a slip of a girl with a pinched mouth. She twirls her black hair around her finger. "Women danced together, back-to-back. Everything was backward."

Shock ripples through the pews.

"The bed's linens were delicate," she adds crisply. "The meadow's flowers delicate, too, like lace."

"Mornings tending the horse I've found her covered with sweat," says Ursa's older brother. "Hagridden, I wonder."

"That girl's a born liar," scoffs the candlemaker. "Just how did the witch collect her? Ursa sleeps in a windowless room."

"She stretched herself thin," Ursa says, naming her schoolteacher, Ida, who is always scribbling secrets in a thick red book. "And slithered down my chimney."

Mette's four-year-old son—easily frightened and excitable—begins squirming in his seat. "Me too," he blurts.

"Quiet," whispers his father. "This isn't pretend."

"You what?" the priest asks. "Someone took you to Blockula?"

"Yes," answers the boy, though he shakes his head no.

"Who among them?"

He sighs, leaning back against the warmth of Mette's chest. "Mama."

"But why go with her? Good boy like you."

"She promised to buy me a new pair of boots."

Mette's eyes grow wild. Her husband holds his hand to the back of her neck as she begins to cough, ragged and racking.

"It's true," she gags, fingers scraping at her tongue.

Her husband pulls their son into his lap.

"I would have spoken sooner, but Satan blocked my throat. My God, forgive me." She wipes her glistening chin. "I still feel it." She strokes her neck. "In my throat, hair thick and coarse as sheep's wool."

"Settle," commands the priest, though all are silent.

He did not force confession from Ursa, the candle-maker's daughter, or Mette's son, or trembling Mette.

The damned, he has found, seep a peaty smell from their pores like drunkards after revelry, no matter their morning scrub. All spring and summer, as the collective bodies warmed together in his pews, he has smelled them—sweet and sharp—the women who fly to Blockula, who thicken the church air. God is good. He wipes his eyes. The tears surprise him, and his shaking hands. Relieved, the priest knows he, too, is good. Later, when the orphans are found strangled behind the barn, goats nosing their bodies, he will tell himself this, remind himself he is not to blame. *Needless*, he will think of their deaths. *Savages*, of whoever did them in.

There is less protest than he planned for when he locks the women inside the church.

The four without marks are permitted to go. Mothers break from daughters, sisters from sisters. There is stew to be cooked for the men's deliberations. Children to be minded.

Old Abel, Catherine's husband of sixty years, is the only one who wishes to stay behind. Sixty years they've shared a bed.

"And did you share one on Blockula?" asks the priest.

"Blockula isn't real," stutters Abel. "It's madness. Anyone can see, there's nothing out there."

"I'll only ask once more."

Catherine shakes her head. "No," she pleads.

"Well?" the priest says sharply.

"I suppose not," Abel answers. He is hesitant, soft-eyed, looking only at her as the doors close behind him.

Ida opens the heavy red journal—once her grand-mother's, then her mother's. To her, it is a prayerbook.

"Look," Mette says. "Even now, Ida conjures spells. Her lips are moving."

"Hush," says Ida, but she lays the book down. It lives inside her.

Through the keyhole, Herfrid spies her brother, standing guard with his hunter's bow. "Maybe I'll shrink down slimmer than the key and slither out," she mumbles, eyeing Mette. "Maybe I'll fly a kneeler to the ceiling and shatter the windows." In stained glass, haloed villagers till soil and harvest hay, casting amber light.

Herfrid's neighbors stare, afraid of her.

But later the women stretch out in the pews to sing psalms together softly, as if putting children to sleep.

*

On the march through the eastern grassland, their fathers and grandfathers and brothers and uncles surround them. And also their sons—those boys over twelve, with newly lanky limbs and acne-stippled cheeks who not long ago stopped seeking comfort for nightmares but still allow their mothers to brush the hair back from their brows. Shy boys, with blank faces. The men carry pitchforks and scythes and pikes and torches and knives. A fire poker and an axe. Abel sneaks hold of Catherine's hand. "Forgive me," he says as she moans. "I tried. I tried." Herfrid hisses, "I'll come back to torment you. Am I not a witch?" Signe's spit streaks her uncle's cheek. "Easy," cautions the priest. "She isn't herself."

The women link arms. They lean on each other's shoulders and sing. The Blue Maiden and the setting sun are behind them, the horizon pink and hazy once more. Cattle low. An infestation of caterpillars has woven cocoons in the branches of every poplar. *On Blockula*, thinks Signe, *I walk a labyrinth that has no end. I never reach its center.* Ida remembers, of all things, her father teaching her to tip honeysuckle blossoms to her mouth for nectar. She waits for their bloom each spring. Now, they scent the air. He limps not far from her on his bad knee. She loves him, still.

"Vengeance will be the Lord's," a mother whispers in her daughter's ear. "The Lord will repay."

Another looks to the sky. "Deliver me. Deliver me."

Abel calls, "Even our sows are stunned before slaughter," at which point he is stunned by the axe handle.

"God is not merciless," says the priest nearing the pyre. "He asks me to save this unborn child."

When he pulls pregnant Signe from the others, she struggles against him. She wants to stay linked with the women. She wears one boot, her left foot bare.

Their throats are slit at a good distance from the wood, so it will be dry enough for the bodies to burn.

That morning, thirty-two women had awoken on the island. Now, there are five.

They stoke coals, soak linens, boil water, brush snarls from the children's hair.

The men and boys are glassy-eyed, but their clothes reek of smoke only until the next washing.

Part II

Berggrund Island, Sweden

1825

Signe gives birth to a daughter, who gives birth to a daughter, who gives birth to a daughter, who gives birth to a son.

The son becomes a priest. Like every Berggrund priest before him, he lives in the tall thin parish house on the island's southern point—still standing five generations later despite weather-worn slats, crooked shutters, and a sunken porch. Silas shares the house with two daughters, six and ten years old. Their names are Beata and Ulrika.

The other children call the house Bloody Windows. Mostly in whispers, but sometimes one will break from the pack walking to the schoolhouse to shout it, tossing pebbles that ping off the fence. The shutters are rusted red by salt spray. Late at night, candlelight flickers in the sisters' third-story room. They wait in the window, looking out.

◊

After weeks of hunting, Bea finds the key hidden beneath the sole of their father's slipper.

As he prepares to give Sunday service, combing water through his disheveled hair, they fake nausea. "You must really be suffering," he says. "To forgo the Sabbath." Bea prays he won't return with the doctor, who palpates their stomachs with tremoring hands.

The key slides easily into the lock. For the first time in six years, the door to their mother's bedroom swings open.

"Are you sure you want to?" asks Ulrika.

When Bea enters, the air is humid and thick, like it is in the woods where the ground grows soft at the edge of the swamp. Everything is coated with dust.

"Look," Bea whispers, dumping baby teeth from a lace pouch into her palm.

"Those teeth were mine," Ulrika says. She riffles through the bedside table drawer, pulling out a round white stone and a red leather-bound book. Bea grips the stone while Ulrika leafs through the book's yellowed pages, pressed violets fluttering to the floor. Over Ulrika's shoulder, Bea glimpses a starfish or maybe a lily.

"Is it a diary?" Bea asks, hopeful.

Ulrika shakes her head. "More of a naturalist's guide."

A long list of women's names are inscribed in the front, but Bea only recognizes *Bruna*, the village herbalist and healer, and beneath that, *Angelique*. Bea is whispering their mother's name when Ulrika closes the cover.

"I'm taking this," she says. "He'll never know."

Bea uncorks a bottle of brown tincture, lip prints on the rim. When Ulrika turns to the dresser, Bea sneaks a swallow and gags. It tastes the way a leather saddle smells.

"Try this on," Ulrika says, holding out a necklace. The island's women never wear jewelry. Inside the blue pendant, a woman's profile is carved in raised ivory stone.

Bea runs her fingertip over its contours. "Is this her?"

"No." Ulrika ties the choker tightly around Bea's neck, the pendant cold and heavy at the base of her throat. "I don't know this woman."

Ulrika snakes her arm into the leg of a black stocking, revealing a jagged run.

The dresses in the armoire are simple, with yellow armpits and frayed hems. Mold blooms at their seams. There is a wool sweater with brass buttons. An empty traveling bag. A long gray coat with spring-green lining. Bea reaches into the pocket and finds a tear in the smooth silk. Her hand slips through the hole.

Deep inside the coat, her fingers close around a small, circular shape that must have slipped through, too.

A silver ring.

The band is etched with N. H. and L. H., unfamiliar initials, neither her mother's nor her father's.

The ring is too big for Bea. She drops it back into its hiding place.

On the coat's collar, a strand of red hair. She winds it tight around her finger, until the tip turns purple and pulses with her heart.

"From when she died?" Bea asks, pointing to a stain on the bed's coverlet.

"Only wine," says Ulrika, who has begun to tremble. "Sometimes she took her meals in bed."

She leads Bea out of the room, hand steadying as she locks the door again.

Their mother died giving birth to Bea.

Once, the doctor told Bea that the joy of his life was pulling newborns from his big black bag.

"Don't you know by now?" he said, patting the bag's cracked leather, the sides swollen, stuffed full. "This is where babies come from."

"A baby can't fit in there," she'd said.

"I thought so, too. But when I reach my hand in, like magic, it's so deep I can fit my whole arm. I bet I could fit my whole self if I had to." He winked. "All the babies I'll ever deliver are in there, cozy and asleep."

When he asked if she wanted to see, she went quiet. He undid the clasp anyway. The bag creaked open. Inside were silver instruments and vials of medicine. He shook the handles, and the tools and pills rattled. "I'm afraid the magic only works for me," he said.

But he had her put her hand in anyway to feel the plain old bottom of the bag, where crumbs collected.

Later, a boy from school shared what his father told him: babies lived inside rotten tree stumps and had to be whittled out.

When she sees the doctor's bag swinging at his side or Boe Henriksson whittling with a bone-handled knife, she is filled with momentary horror, the queasy feeling that dawns at the beginning of a bad dream.

◊

Her father lets Bea up into his lap, a rare treat.

Most days he locks himself in his study to read gospel, write sermons, and fast, only emerging for occasional bowls of Ulrika's thin porridge, staring over their heads to some distant place. He says he's an old man, with little time left for devotion. Though he is fifty, he looks much younger than the other old men with long beards and mottled cheeks. All night, Bea hears his murmurs below, urgent but indiscernible confessions to God. The Holy Spirit tells him to deny his body's feeble desires. "Did you do something wrong?" Bea asked once, for if she stumbles reciting the Lord's Prayer she is supposed to go hungry. But Ulrika, who cooks, always sneaks Bea a plateful. "We've all done terrible things," he answered. "I may be the worst of sinners. My whole life is repentance." But only faith redeems sins, he reminded her. By faith, through Christ, they are forgiven. They live in grace. "No, I offer my wakefulness, my hunger, as a gift," he'd said, smiling. "To God. A show of love. For the undeserved love he shows me." Bea's father has never told her he loves her, and she does not know how to make him smile. Even God is not exempt from her jealousy, when it flares.

19

Straw crosses are propped on his windowsill. His desk is scattered with papers, his sweater tea stained. He missed dinner but chews peppercorns, kept alert by a burning tongue.

"Which of us is most like Mother?" Bea risks, a question she's been holding for a moment alone with him, though she's afraid he'll put her down. They are not supposed to talk about her mother.

His dark eyebrows furrow.

"She was like me," he says softly. "We were both curious."

Bea leans her cheek against him, his sweater itchy, his heart pounding. She snaps off a loose button for Ulrika to mend.

"I meant me or Ulrika."

"Neither of you."

She still has the strand of her mother's hair, a red that streaks their own dark blond only after months in the sun.

"You might look a bit like her," he concedes. "But Ulrika behaves like her, time to time."

"Like a beast."

"Certainly. A beast." His breath is peppery. "With Viking blood."

"I wish she had a portrait," Bea sighs. "Do you think I could be beautiful like her when I grow up?"

Though her eyes are different colors—one blue and one brown—she feels, for the moment, sure he'll say yes. The study is filled with soft, warm light. She fits her hand into his and their shapes are just the same. She could fall asleep right there, to his voice rumbling in his chest.

"Who told you she was beautiful?"

"Ulrika."

He slides her from his lap, spins her, and glances at her. The inspection is quick, still her cheeks burn.

"Your mother was captivating," he says, eyes shining. "She knew it. And suffered for it. Be glad you inherited my plain little face."

"She looked like me," says Ulrika when Bea brings her the same question.

Like a beast, Bea wants to say but won't. "Well, who did she behave like?"

"Me," Ulrika says.

"You were only four when she died," says their father, glancing up from his Bible. "You don't remember." Ulrika stares back, unblinking. "I remember being born," she says, like a threat.

There are things Bea has forgotten. But now she is six and determined to remember everything.

◊

When the wind gusts, Bea feels their bedroom sway. Outside the window there is only moonlit meadow overgrown with sumac, the white froth of the elder tree they like to hide in, and the curving road. Beyond it, the glint of ocean. There is no view of the Blue Maiden.

21

Helmi growls, and Bea runs the dog's velvety ear between her fingers. Their father paces the study below, praying. She does not know if he ever sleeps.

Hours later, she wakes sweat drenched and towels off with her nightgown. Whenever Bea is awake, Ulrika is, too. Bea does not know what woke them, until the woman's laughter sounds again, just outside the window.

"She's here," Bea says. Finally. Finally.

"Only the tavern letting out," says Ulrika. Bea tallies what lies between their house and the tavern: grocer, butcher, wharf.

She begs to hear the legend once more. It scares her in a way she craves. Telling it, Ulrika's voice turns slow and deep, like their music box when its key winds down.

Children wake to the sound of fingertips on the windowpane. It makes no difference if they sleep four stories up. The witch finds them.

Sometimes, it seems the story takes place long ago.

Other times, the woman's face might be hovering, just out of view, in the dark.

"Who is she?" Bea asks.

"Who do you think?" answers Ulrika. "She's who you least expect. She could be your own mother. Your own sister." She yanks down the blanket that covers Bea's ear and nibbles on her earlobe.

Ulrika's left ear is crumpled, but she's promised Bea it was normal when she was born. Then at four years old she woke to a woman bent over her ear, whispering wetly before taking a bite.

"What did she say?" Bea had asked.

"Run."

Because Ulrika is almost eleven, Bea believes everything her sister tells her. She pulls her head through her collar. Inside the safe tent of her nightgown, she breathes the onion smell of her own breath. She watches her stomach rise and fall, soft and round.

She knows when her mother arrives at the window, she'll have a long, thin braid just like Bea's and dirt under her nails. Her fingertips on the glass will sound like the ticking of rain, and Bea will climb out to her.

Circumnavigate.

It is Ulrika's word. When Bea finally wraps her mouth around its syllables, she feels powerful and brave and older, not herself. It is July. The sun sets late, and the tide is low. The seaweed jumps with sand fleas.

She knows Berggrund's creeks and pond, the estuary and the dank beneath its bridge, the black rock beaches harborside and the sandy shores facing open water. And she's learned some island history, classroom lessons: burial grounds, Viking rune stones, the witch trial, and vague battles, grave markers honoring centuries of fallen fathers and sons. In Berggrund's woodland she's straddled gnarled pines with trunks misshapen by wind, some charred by lightning strikes. Among them, Bea cannot help but whisper.

Each day she walks the island's sole main road to school, which winds along the coast, between the neat row of houses and the grassland. She passes the church and celebration hall, working windmills and those with broken wings. Beyond the schoolhouse lies the great alvar, scorched-looking land of scrub and limestone, empty except for sheep, cairns, and the Holmberg farm.

Alongside Ulrika, she's even trekked Berggrund end to end, from her doorstep to the North Cliffs, home sunburnt and blistered by midafternoon. But until now she's never thought to walk the island all the way around.

Determined, she whispers, "Circumnavigate."

"I'll mind what I say," says Ulrika. "You'll latch on to anything."

They cross under the pier, its poles slippery with sea moss, fishermen above hauling in the day's last catch.

"Hurry," Ulrika says.

At the cove's edge, they climb a ladder of exposed roots and whack through scrub brush, skittering back down in slick-bottomed boots.

The next stretch of beach is all boulders and granite slabs, waves lapping like animals at a trough. Bea chants *circumnavigate* in her head. She scrapes her palms on barnacles. They scramble from rock to rock. Bea keeps her head down, intent only on following the course her sister winds.

At last, Ulrika stops. "We're trapped," she says.

Before them, the incoming tide has eaten their path. Surf crashes on the shore. Behind them, their route is underwater.

"I'm climbing up," says Ulrika.

"That's cheating," Bea says, as her sister fits her toe into a crevice. The shale crumbles. On the beach outside their house, they climb easily into a shallow cave, hiding two dolls with shriveled apples for heads.

"We have to turn back," says Ulrika. "I made a mistake."

"No," Bea says. "We're close."

In truth, she doesn't quite know where they are. She can still see the distant dock, empty now, jutting out behind them. If they could scale the bank, she suspects they wouldn't be too far from home, Mikael Lofgren's pasture, maybe, or Bruna's hut on the edge of the bluffs, the embankment it is built on eroding bit by bit each winter.

"I'm going on," says Bea. Instead she sits down, raking her nails through orange lichen.

"We could never have made it around," Ulrika says. "Past the North Cliffs. You must have known that."

Her sister starts back without her.

But Bea waits on the rock until the waves wash over her boots.

When Ulrika returns for her, she yanks Bea's arm. It will bruise. "Now," she commands. Somehow, already, it is dusk.

They're forced to wade into the water, calf-deep and freezing. Each step is impossibly slow, rocked by the current. The tide rises to Bea's thighs, then her chest. Ulrika grips her hand. Bea is just learning to swim.

When the water laps Bea's mouth, she slings her arms around her sister's neck. Their skirts billow up. For brief stretches, Ulrika's feet don't touch bottom, and she paddles with Bea on her back.

At last there is a clear route to clamber up. Bea's body is numb, her legs wobbling. She watches them carry her down the empty street. Her legs might as well not belong to her. Her teeth chatter. Her dress is chafing and heavy, pockets gritty with sand.

They reach their gate just after dark. In the upstairs window, their father writes at his desk. He never seems to notice when they're gone.

"We're spirits now," Ulrika says. "We drowned. We can never go back inside."

◊

All summer, they play at being shipwrecked.

Bea can still feel the wet dress dragging, her hair snarled and stiff with salt water, her fingers fumbling and bloodless. This is how girls look when they survive and wash up on the shore.

The island they are stranded on is uninhabitable, like the Blue Maiden.

They are forced to live on mealy bugs that scuttle from overturned stumps. Bea swallows one like a pill.

In the middle of the grassland sits an abandoned skiff, its hull soft with rot. This is the boat they are tossed from. Helmi sprints through the meadow alongside them. Later, Bea will groom her fur—warm from the fire—for burs and ticks swollen with blood.

By August, they have scabbed elbows, callused feet, scalps itchy with sand. In silty stretches of loam, purple orchids shiver, their blossoms like tongues. The cover of their mother's red book is threadbare at the edges, the pages stained and creased. Ulrika studies what is safe to eat. They nibble mushrooms with woody stems, bitter thyme from the heath. They steep moss in pond water cupped in their hands and call it tea.

At low tide, they rip seaweed pods open with their teeth. The pads of their fingers and toes prune. They pluck periwinkles from tide pools and crush them. Gnarled apple trees grow along the bank, full of juice and only the occasional worm. Salt sprayed, the apples taste like a summer storm.

◊

Then comes November. A world of snow.

A snowdrift traps six of Nilla Holmberg's flock of sheep. By the time they are discovered and dug out, all but one is frozen. Nilla leads the ewe that lived around the grassland on a bristly rope. When Bea passes by, Nilla grips her shoulder. "This old girl ate the fleece of the ones she was buried under." She says it to all who will listen. "Eight whole days, she lived on nothing but wool. A miracle."

◊

While their father saws ice, Helmi skitters off across the bay, dashing toward the edge where freeze melts into choppy water. Ulrika puts her fingers in her cheeks, her whistle shrill. All along the shoreline, men look up from their ice holes.

"When I was a boy," their father says, "the whole bay froze, clear to the mainland." The few stories he does tell, Bea has heard before. At every funeral he preaches of a boat disappearing over one horizon, appearing in the distance on another.

He claims winters were more brutal, back then. Islanders could cross the length of ice in half a day, and dozens of them did. It was too thick for fishing holes—for the saw's blade.

He pauses to give Bea one of his gloves. She has forgotten her mittens. She stuffs both hands inside it, the fleece lining matted and warm. Then he's sawing again, knuckles red and wet with ice melt.

"One day my friend's father decided to hitch up his horses to ride a carriage across. We stood on the shore to watch him go, cheering. The horses wore tinkling bells."

People were still cheering when the ice broke. There must have been a warmer channel, he tells them, out in the bay's center. No one understood precisely how it happened. The carriage fell through, and then the horses. And of course, the driver.

"I remember Ma walking me out onto the ice," interrupts Ulrika.

"People ran to help," he says over the saw's rhythmic rasp. "There was shouting. My mother wouldn't let me join. It must have been a mile out or more. My father tried to take his horse, but the horse bucked. Just as well. He wasn't thinking clearly."

"She pulled me in a sled," Ulrika says.

The saw jams.

"Helmi came with us," says Ulrika.

"Of course she did." He is breathing hard. The teeth are stuck, the blade wobbling. "For one day, let's not talk about your mother. How about that?" He lifts his hand to scratch Helmi under her gray muzzle. "Our stout protector," he says. "Our good girl."

"Ma wrapped me in sheepskins," Ulrika says. "She wore a gray coat."

"You don't remember her." He jerks the handle. "You would have been a baby."

"We walked so far out we could look back and see the whole shore," says Ulrika. "But the ice didn't go all the way across. We went up to the edge."

Bea shuts her eyes. She can see her mother's small shape, the long stretch of ice behind her. The hood of the coat hides her face.

"I remember, too," says Bea.

"Lord, help us," says her father, clenching and un-clenching his hand. "Don't you start."

Bruna opens the door to her hut without a word, as if she's been waiting on them.

It is another room that they are not supposed to enter. Inside, the stone walls are black with lichen. Dried flowers hang from the beams, and the shelves are lined with liquids and powders. The room encroaches on Bea, home to the smell that trails Bruna: unguents and incense. Something boils on the stove. Bea peers into the pot of silty dark water, debris dredged from the stream.

"Only breakfast," says Bruna. "Dandelion greens." She wears men's trousers and a broad-brimmed straw hat low over her eyes. The other children whisper that Bruna gained healing power by eating a sacred white snake whole and alive, her red hair sapped of color overnight. Now there are two white braids down her back. But their father dismisses this rumor. While he was preparing for priesthood, Bruna was merely a sly little girl, slow at her lessons. He'd have them know there are no sacred snakes or unearned powers and that islanders who believe such things—instead of trusting their university-trained doctor or priest—are simpleminded and stuck in the past.

*

31

"I suspect you know about the day the women burned," Bruna says when Ulrika pulls the red book from her satchel to ask why Bruna's name is inside it. "Children tend to know such things."

For Bea, that day—like all history—is too far removed to feel real. What matters is its lore: *Be good, or the witch will take you.*

"My great-great-grandmother Ursa was eight years old then." Bruna eyes an empty chair by the fire as if the girl sits with them. "She testified in church her teacher flew her to Blockula. The next day, her teacher was gone. And Ursa's mother was gone. And her aunt, too. And her grandmother." Bruna halts. "She begged forgiveness in the empty church and found this book in the pew."

Ursa's brother stopped speaking for seven years, until one day he threw himself from the North Cliffs. But Ursa lived and lived and lived, and her guilt, with the red book, was passed down daughter to daughter.

"Until it arrived at me. But I'm too busy for guilt. And I'll have no daughters. So I gave it to Angelique." She lays a hand on the book's cover, which takes up the whole of Ulrika's lap. "She would have passed it on to you one day. I'm glad you found it." She swings it open. The spine is beginning to crack and mold grows along the hinge.

Bruna says the name Angelique unflinchingly, as she says Blockula.

At home, they do not speak their mother's name, or if they do, they whisper.

Their mother was a mainlander.

Bruna tells them how Angelique's love of plants began in her own mother's garden, in the middle of the city. Her first memory was kneeling in dirt with worms. Carriages slowed to take in winding paths of dahlias and lilacs. She hummed as she drew buds, then open petals and bees.

Her school trained girls in botany so they might charm at dinners, revere God's majesty, and have pink cheeks. "After all, trouble comes from overexploring the interior world." Bruna winks. "Angelique learned the name for everything. Once she could name something, she could see it, and then she saw it everywhere."

Bea cannot yet read. She is just learning to see and name the world around her. When she tries to picture the garden, a blur of color blooms in her mind. But her mother's form stays hazy.

"When Angelique's mother fell sick, her garden went wild," Bruna says. Passersby gaped at the weeds, thorns, and vines. "They traveled to Berggrund for a summer of healing. Seaside air, swims. Doctor's orders. Back then the inn was open. Angelique was meant to nurse her. None of it helped. But Angelique came alive here. Seventeen, the whole island was her garden. She left her mother on the shore. She couldn't stop herself."

People stared from their porches as she cut through private pasture, Helmi an unleashed puppy barking at cattle. She scaled stone walls guarded by blackthorn that sliced her ankles, sketching and cataloguing. She was the first to identify the red helleborine orchid, its petals like a gull in flight, and the carnivorous alpine butterwort, and velvet night coral bells. Hours each day she crisscrossed the alvar, until Bruna took up her birch basket to join her.

"We taught each other what we could," Bruna says.

Bruna knew plants by other names, island names: pestilence daisy, psalm berry, healing tongue, and trembling grass. Ida's flower, and Gudrun's, and Signe's, namesakes long dead. She taught Angelique that devil's bit dyed cloth a pale green and sweet flag root tea soothed the spirit. Small pleasures.

"I might have taught her how to go unnoticed," Bruna says. "As if that were possible. You should know, her mind was a marvel. She'd memorized her field guides. She told me that Berggrund's nothing like the mainland. Warmer winter, cooler summer. Windswept, of course. A miracle, she said, all that thrives here. Life you can't find on the mainland, and our only rich, deep soil the church graveyard. She liked the orchids best." Bruna waves her hand at the smoke-filled room. "I never thought this place so special. But then I've never left."

As she thumbs through the book, Berggrund's world flips past in ink and watercolor—bilberry, fiddleheads, and ferns, bulbs putting out shoots. "She had an eye," Bruna says. "She put it all down in the book. Here's my favorite."

She runs a fingertip across a drawing of leaves riddled with holes, the caterpillar that chewed them, the cocoon, the hatching butterfly, and a rook with the butterfly's wings snapped in her beak, offered up to peeping chicks.

"Things changed, after her mother died," Bruna says. "She blamed herself."

"And then she married our father?" asks Bea.

"That she did." Bruna hesitates. "I doubt he'd like you coming here, but you always can."

The rest of the pages are blank. Bruna snaps the cover shut. "I'll tell you what I told her. Fill them."

◊

In the red book's earliest passages, those Bruna did not mention, ornate script grows shaky, blotched, and bent. Ulrika teases Bea with spells and warnings she refuses to share. "Let me keep something to myself," she insists. "This part will only scare you."

But tonight is Maundy Thursday, when Satan possessed Judas, and evil but also magic is most powerful, so Ulrika has a spell they must try together.

Like all island children on the eve of Long Friday, they disguise themselves as witches. Tomorrow they will dress in mourners' black and prick their fingers harvesting rosehips for crimson soup, a reminder of Christ's blood and crown. Bea can hear the faint screams of the others as they march from house to house, the bonfires already burning. Soon all the good treats will be gone. Last year, half the neighbors locked their doors and shuttered the windows. Bea and Ulrika came home with kettles half-full of Bruna's wild pears, tins of throat lozenges from the grocer, and sugar skulls hard as granite gifted by Widow Ingrid, leftovers from her husband's recent funeral, inedible though Bea sucked them for their sweetness.

Ulrika paints beetroot circles on their cheeks. With a lump of coal, she dots black freckles over the bridge of Bea's nose, then her own. They snatch up copper kettles and brooms, pounding the ceiling that is the floor of their father's study with the handles to tell him they are off, no response but a dusting of silt shaken loose. He spends this day and night in prayer but allows them to go for what he calls a bit of silliness he cannot put a stop to.

Ulrika carries a lantern. She tucks the red book and a knife into her waistband. Helmi, in place of a black cat, trails them.

At the estuary, Elias Axelsson straddles a bough that grows over the water, which flows and burbles after months of ice still lingering in the harbor. His legs dangle, bare feet swishing ripples.

"Why aren't you with the others?" he asks.

"Why aren't you?" Bea says, though Elias, with his oddity and frequent spells of illness, is most often alone.

Even his older twin brothers, Samuel and Erik, tend to avoid him. At least Bea and Ulrika have each other. Their father tells them they are outsiders because they are priest's daughters. He says this as if he is not the priest he speaks of but a different, simpler father.

Elias shrugs. "They left me behind. I'd rather be here."

He is uncostumed, in the same velvet overcoat he wears every day, even in the height of summer, which hides the gentle curve of his spine and uneven shoulders. When he swims with his older twin brothers, he stays submerged to the neck. His features, too, are faintly crooked, some too large and others too small. Their classmates whisper how his looks are proof of his parents' hidden sins, like lecherous Farmer Larson's two-headed calf or Bruna's bleached, shimmery hair.

"Found it," Ulrika says, sifting pebbles from the streambed. She holds up a piece of yellowish rock. "Sulfur. We're casting a spell," she tells Elias before Bea can protest. She had thought the spell a secret just for them. "You should come with us. It's more powerful with three."

The sky is the bright blue it turns just before dark, bats darting overhead.

"Fine," Bea sighs as Elias climbs down to join them. "But if you're coming, you have to dress up." He lets her wrap him in her shawl. He is the only child her age smaller than she is. She ties her apron around his narrow waist and her kerchief under his chin. His eyelashes are so long they brush against his glasses. His cheeks are flushed red, as if he, too, were painted. "There," she says, "pretty," and is surprised to see it's true.

Ulrika leads them back to their own field.

"Read to me," Ulrika says, handing Elias the red book, open to the spell. He does not ask where they found such a thing, squinting in the last light. Unlike Bea, he has been reading for years. "To reveal the dead. To bring them back." Bea repeats the words just after he speaks them, pretending she knows them, too, and they share the same breath.

"Take sulfur stone ground to powder." Ulrika crushes the sulfur against a nearby boulder, brushing its dust into her palm. "Mix well with the fuel of your lamp." Bea worries the powder will blow away as Ulrika pours it into the oil, swishing the two together. "At nightfall, light the wick." Ulrika strikes her match. The flame wavers. "What next?" she whispers. Elias reads, "Carve the name of the one you miss into their old doorstep."

While Ulrika is gone, Bea and Elias go quiet, their breathing synched as they stare at the guttering candle. Helmi lies at Bea's feet. The field shushes around them. The last of the sun goes down.

Ulrika comes running back. "It's done."

"Now say, *Return, return, return*, as many times as you can before the flame dies."

"Together," Ulrika says.

"Return, return, return," the three of them chant. "Return, return, return."

"Keep going," urges Ulrika. Their voices blend into one.

The flame snuffs out.

In the sudden, quiet dark, Bea's laughter is soft, nearly to herself.

She listens as the laugh grows louder. She hides her face. Laughing tightens the same muscles around her mouth and eyes as crying. Her face twists behind her hands. When she begins to sob, Elias shakes her shoulder and says, "Come back."

Whatever gripped her lets her go.

She dries her tears on her sleeve.

"I think a demon tried to get inside you," Ulrika says, cupping Bea's face in her hands. "But now it's gone."

"What did it want?" Bea asks.

"To steal your energy," says Ulrika. "To make itself stronger. So it could appear, in her place."

They trudge back to their doorstep with empty kettles.

If the intruder is secreted away inside her, leaching from her, she cannot find it. Toes to scalp, there is only a tingling where her attention roves, as if her blood fizzes.

"I saw them," Elias whispers to Bea. "The ghosts. But then, I always do."

*

Ulrika pounds the door. Bea is afraid to look down and see the fresh carving on the frame, afraid and hopeful, too, that her mother will answer their knocking after all. Returned to them. She closes her eyes and batters her fists and the wood shakes. Helmi yips. They stamp and hoot, beat their brooms against the windows, clang their kettles, and at last their father whips the door open to growl, "Get off my porch, I've nothing for you." But recognizing them, his scowl softens. "Girls?" he says. "And is that Elias? I don't think you're supposed to visit your own house."

And Ulrika shouts, "We're not your girls, we're witches." And Bea joins in, "Not your girls, not us, not Ulrika, not Bea," until he disappears inside in search of something he can give them.

When spring thaws the bay, a pale head bobs above the waves.

It moves toward them, making quick time, gliding past the boats anchored in the harbor.

They've been warned of coyotes swimming across in stealthy packs from the mainland. But they have never seen one. Only scat and scattered feathers, spines and beaks that once were gulls.

Now the creature is close enough that they can see its long ears, alert and swiveling.

"A deer," Ulrika sighs. She picks up a gray stone and chucks it toward the animal, just missing its neck.

"Don't," says Bea, but her sister scoops up another. When the next stone grazes the deer, she swerves but keeps on swimming, huffing as she paddles.

"Go home," Ulrika shouts.

"Stop," Bea grabs Ulrika's arm. "What's wrong with you?"

"They'll hunt her."

The deer climbs from the shallows on legs thin as stilts. Unsteadily, she picks her way across the rocks, water coursing down her fur.

Her tongue licks at the air as if in search of leaves.

She bounds up the beach into lupine, the white of her tail arcing through blossoms.

They are in the schoolhouse when the gunshot sounds.

Bea tells the teacher her stomach aches. To her surprise, she is believed. "You look like you've seen a ghost," Teacher says, permitting her to go home early. Ulrika raises her eyebrows, mouthing, "Told you so," as Bea passes her desk.

Bea balances along the stone wall that snakes through Boe Henriksson's gardens, trespassing the lots behind the houses instead of walking the road, arms teetering. Something white pokes from the tilled earth. She digs up a slim jawbone. The sun warms her hair. Rivulets of water trickle. At the edge of Boe's field, cows munch juniper. There is no sign of the deer, still Bea looks for her.

She steals a milkweed pod, furred and soft as an animal's ear.

At the mouth of her drive, she kicks off her shoes and rolls down her stockings. After the winter, her feet are tender.

Poppy buds crowd the front gate, her father's favorite flower. She slices the green open with her thumbnail. Inside, red petals are crumpled and damp. She unfolds them.

From a distance, it might look like the first true bloom.

Tucked against the porch pillar is a bird's nest with three cracked blue eggs, whatever grew in them hatched or stolen.

She takes this, too.

Already, the name carved in the sill has begun to fade. If her father noticed it as he stepped over it, he never said.

Her mother's things seem to have shifted since Bea last unlocked the door.

She calls out, "Hello," as she's done in each empty room. No one is home, though the sole of her father's slipper is warm.

She puts the poppy in the empty vase and the nest on the window frame. Beside the tincture, her milkweed pod spills its downy seeds. Of all the things in her mother's room, it is the simple white stone in the bedside drawer that has lingered in Bea's mind. She does not know why. She weighs the stone in her palm, and it warms against her. She slips it into her pocket. These offerings can take its place. Though she wanted to drop the jawbone through the tear in the coat's lining in exchange for the hidden ring, she feels suddenly, terribly tired. Instead, she tucks it under the mattress and lies down. Her stomach aches after all.

When she wakes, the ache is gone and the sun is low.

The house is quiet.

Carefully, she tidies the covers and brushes her hair. In the bristles her dull strands twine with her mother's red.

Her father is waiting in the hall. Her breath catches. She wants to run back into the room. Instead, she freezes.

"My key," he says, holding out his hand.

Ivar Andersson delivers a cut of venison.

"Can't have them nibbling away at our gardens," he says to her father, smiling at Bea over his shoulder.

That night, Ulrika ladles out stew.

Their father gives thanks, then tells them it's time Bea and Ulrika stop sharing a bed.

"Children should learn to be alone," he says, tearing his bread. "It's hard enough growing up, without being packed tight together like puppies."

Bea might be sick. She pushes back her chair, and it tips over.

"Young lady," their father says.

She lies down with Helmi on the hearth, resting her head on the soft fur of her belly. The dog's legs kick, giving chase in a dream.

◊

The next day, returning from school, they spot smoke.

The back field is charred.

From inside, Bea watches their father tend coals in the drizzle, minding the last of the flames.

She falls asleep without supper on the settee as Ulrika reads, and wakes up held in her father's arms. "Put me down," she almost says but doesn't. She has just turned seven. He has not carried her to bed in years. Her limbs go heavy. He smells of the fire, stale and sour.

There is light under the door to her mother's room. He nudges it open.

Everything is gone.

The room is chill with spring air. The curtain blows back and forth.

"You like it so well in here," he says. "Now it's yours."

It's not true that nothing is left. There is still the bed, the side table, the empty armoire, and the dresser cleared of its vase, mirror, and brush. The dust is polished and the floor swept.

In the lamplight, the room's dark wood gleams.

The coverlet has been changed to a quilt, each square familiar, fabric cut from their old dresses.

"What were you burning?" she asks.

He lays her down.

In a gentler voice, he says, "Why have a lovely big bed, in the loveliest room in the house, if none of us use it?"

Without her mother's things, the room is vast and strange. "I don't want it," she whispers.

"Be grateful. By rights it should be Ulrika's."

He tucks her in, brushing back her hair. She closes her eyes as he kneels. He thanks God for keeping them both another day and prays He keeps them through the night.

She is afraid of the empty drawers, the empty armoire. She is afraid of the bed her mother died in. She pats her pocket in secret. All day, she has reached for the stone. It is still there. He has not taken it, too. She hopes the red book is safe with Ulrika.

"Let Your holy angel be with us," he finishes, "that the evil foe may have no power over us."

After he goes, she senses Ulrika waiting on the other side of the door, but when she checks no one is there.

Back in bed, she hears Helmi scratching to be let in. But again, the hall is empty.

"What is your name?" Ulrika asks.

Around Bea, the upstairs bedroom materializes in moonlit dark. Her sister sits up in bed, curls wild.

"What is your name?" she asks again.

"Ulrika," she guesses. A garbled sound comes from her mouth, as if she speaks underwater.

The world wavers, muted and blurry.

"Wake up," Ulrika says.

At breakfast, Ulrika will laugh about Bea sleepwalking, how she came stumbling in.

Only then, fragments from the night shake loose.

How she left her mother's room to walk the hallway, knocking on each closed door: broom closet, library, her father's study. He did not answer, but his floorboards creaked.

In her memory, all is green tinged as she takes the narrow stairs, each step unnaturally labored, like she walks against a current.

She knocks and knocks and knocks.

*

Bea digs the gooseberry from her steaming bowl of oatmeal. Every morning, Helmi sits at Bea's feet in expectation of a gooseberry, her eyebrows worrying. But today, she hasn't come.

She checks the hearth. She checks the rooms upstairs. She climbs down into the root cellar.

"I haven't seen her since yesterday," says Ulrika.

Bea carries the gooseberry onto the porch. She circles the house, calling. Boots crunching through the burned grass, she bends to pick up something glinting gold in the ashes. An earring. There is more. A scrap of fabric. A brass button, like the ones on her mother's sweater. She runs back to Ulrika, soot on her hands.

"Try your whistle," Bea says.

"Dogs run off sometimes," says Ulrika. "They come back."

Bea slides on her stomach to look beneath the porch, where the barn cat hid when he got sick. She tries to remember the last time she saw Helmi. She thinks of the scratching at her door.

"Did they hunt her?" she asks and begins to cry.

"Of course not." Ulrika claps her hands, calling. "It's an island. How lost can she be?"

Bea rides Ulrika's shoulders to the schoolhouse, thighs shaking. She is afraid of her new height and holds her body rigid when it wants to sway. She watches the crooked white line of Ulrika's part, scanning the roadside in furtive glimpses.

The Blue Maiden hunches on the bay's horizon like an animal bedded down. *Blockula*, thinks Bea, then she worries she has said the name aloud.

Behind them, their schoolmates chase a flock of sheep escaped from pasture to the rocks. The sheep bleat, their hooves slipping on seaweed.

Ulrika has grown taller than the boys her age and nearly as broad shouldered, while Bea stays small. She grips gently to the tip of her sister's braid, a lead, but when a gust blows off the ocean she clamps her hands over Ulrika's eyes or ears or mouth. She can't help it, though Ulrika bats her away. There's nowhere else to hold.

They pass the rushes, brittle stalks hissing together in the breeze, taller than the sisters combined.

Bea points out a path trampled through them, but Ulrika's long-legged stride ferries them swiftly past.

"Go back," Bea says. "I think Helmi's in there."

"She's not," says Ulrika.

When Bea begs to be let down, the ground feels unsteady, as if she's disembarked a boat and hasn't found her land legs.

"We're late," Ulrika says, though much of their class will be, too, ambling down the road behind them, kicking up dust. The sheep crowd together on the ledge, a blur of fleece. "I'm going ahead," Ulrika says.

The path into the rushes is well worn, just wide enough for one body. Reeds scrape against Bea's dress. The path ends in a clearing where the reeds are snapped and stamped flat, as if something fought there, rutted, or slept. She calls for Helmi. The rustle of the dog, whipping through tall grass, surrounds her, but it is only the wind.

◊

When Bea sneaks back up to Ulrika's room, she doesn't bother knocking.

"What's your name?" Ulrika asks. In the moonlight Ulrika's feet poke from the quilt, looking newly long and thin.

"Bea," she says. "I'm awake."

Already, the room's dimensions have warped like they do in Bea's dreams, settings recognizable as themselves but not quite themselves, almost imperceptibly altered. It is as if, in her absence, the room woke and stretched.

She crosses through its shadows, lifts a corner of the covers.

49

"Won't you ask permission?" Ulrika says. "To sleep in my bed?" But her face softens. She slides over, pulling Bea into the warmth where she had lain. The bed, as always, is bitter smelling and full of grit.

"I can't sleep," Bea says, dangling her hand to pat Helmi. Her fingers graze the carpet. The absence is startling. "You still have her book, right? He didn't take that, too?"

"It's here."

"Read to me? Or tell me a story."

Ulrika begins, "One day, a day that seemed like any other, the women of Berggrund Island woke and went to church." Ulrika yawns. "It's too late for this story. It's too long."

But when Bea pleads Ulrika slides the red book, thicker than their father's heavy Bible, from her bedside table drawer. She puts her arm around Bea. In the moon's blue glow, Bea squints at the drawings. "Slower." Bea thumbs back to the beginning. "What does this say?"

"Beware."

"Beware of what?"

"Beware the shadow-being," she reads, "a wraith who walks as your antipode through an underground world, the soles of her feet attached to yours as if sewn together."

The bottoms of Bea's feet tingle as Ulrika flips forward again. "Here's what we need. Elderflower: puts restless children to sleep with its smoke."

"Can't I borrow it?"

"You hardly know one plant from another. You wouldn't understand it."

"I do," Bea protests, but her sister shushes her and hides the book back in its drawer. "What else do you have of hers?"

Ulrika hesitates, then reaches into her pillowcase for the bag of baby teeth. She shakes some into her palm, rolling them delicately, as a jeweler would pearls.

"I have her necklace, too," Ulrika whispers. "Her coat."

Bea imagines Ulrika finding the tear in the pocket and the hidden ring. Her sister's hands are too big, red knuckled. She would only rip the hole wider, reaching in.

"It's not fair," Bea says. "All I have is her stone. I want the coat."

"It won't fit."

"It will," says Bea. "Someday."

Bea thought she would feel safe again, if only she could lie next to her sister. It has been days now without sleep. Instead, the room's furniture and objects seem to inch closer in the dark, leaning over her as if listening or whispering. Each silhouette is known to her—dresser, hatstand, rocking chair, broom, Ulrika's robe hanging limp from the peg on the door. She curls against Ulrika's back, pulling the blanket over her ear.

"Don't ever leave, alright?"

"I wouldn't," says Ulrika. And then, "We can leave together. Flip onto your stomach."

The mattress pressed to Bea's cheek is as lumpy as the ground and faintly damp, stuffed with horsehair.

"Close your eyes," Ulrika says, her voice unwinding deep and slow, and Bea waits for the story of children waking to the woman outside their window, but instead her sister says, "Here's how Ma put me to sleep. You're not lying in bed. You're lying on the back of an animal."

When Ulrika tells the story of the woman coming to take them away, Bea likes to interrupt, "Tell me again what she flies on." And Ulrika will quickly list, as if it makes no difference: a horse, a goat, a sheep, a cow. She'll pause. "Or the body of a snoring man." Then it is Bea's turn to ask, "But where does she take them, the children?" though Bea knows where.

"Do you see what you are riding?" Ulrika asks. "Just let it hold you. Feel it under you."

"I'm riding Helmi," says Bea, though she doesn't see it. The mattress muffles her words.

"Bigger than Helmi. Wilder. It lives in the forest. It walks through the dark."

There's nothing like that on the island. The forest is too small to get lost in. Bea sneaks a look at Ulrika, face down beside her, eyes squinched shut.

"What do you ride?"

"A bear," Ulrika sighs.

"Me too," says Bea.

The words are lost in the warm fur of its neck. It is a bear's coat, coarse and musky, threaded with dust.

52

Bea's body begins to sway, as the giant one beneath her sways.

"What did our mother ride?" she mumbles.

"Nothing," says Ulrika.

But Bea can feel the heat of the three of them together, lined up on the curve of the bear's broad back, as it carries them deeper into the woods.

Their father creaks the stairs, whistling, tone-deaf like Bea. The forest is gone, and the bear with it. The room returns and presses in.

"Girls?" he says, peering around the doorframe as if afraid of what he'll see. "Giggling beasts." He never comes up to the third floor. In the shivering lantern light, his hair sticks out like he has been tugging it, as he does when he can't think, and he can't think when they're awake. He wears the same wrinkled pants and sweater from the daytime, clothing he has worn for many days. He sits on the foot of the bed, at the very edge.

They close their eyes, pretending sleep.

"Beata," he says. "Go back to your room." She slivers her eyes open. "You forget. You're like the top bunk, and I'm the bottom bunk. I hear every whisper."

But it can't be true. Because if he did, he would know their mother's book was hiding in the drawer, and he would take it away.

"I'm scared."

"And why is that?" he says. "Ulrika? I hear the stories you tell."

"Just let her stay," says Ulrika.

54

"You seem to relish scaring her."

"We all know what happens to bad girls who disobey their fathers." Ulrika pokes Bea's ribs. "A witch will come and fly us to Blockula."

Bea flinches. "Don't say that name."

"My dear," he says. "We are a family of faith, not superstition."

"Maybe you could sing us to sleep," suggests Ulrika. "One last night together."

"Me? Sing?" His voice is soft with surprise.

"You used to sing to me," Ulrika says. "I remember that, too."

He has never sung for Bea. "You'd like that?" He clears his throat. "What song did I sing?"

"'Now the Time of Blossoming Arrives,'" says Ulrika, and the scattered notes he whistled on the stairs assemble themselves for Bea into this song. It's one she knows.

"I sang that when I was a boy," he says. "I don't remember the words."

She expects him, then, to choose one of the plodding hymns from church. Instead, he begins, in a high, quiet voice, "Again Thy Glorious Sun Doth Rise," which is what they sing at school for Morning Prayer. His voice shakes. She is filled with dread at the sudden thought that she might laugh, an urge that seizes her and Ulrika at the worst moments: funerals and burials. She bites the inside of her cheek. The moon is reflected in his glasses, twin winks of white. Outside, it is still dark, but the birds know otherwise and are singing, too.

He wakes them when the sun comes up, the compass around his neck. He is taking them on a picnic.

The compass lives in his desk, in a little wooden chest lined with black velvet that fits its form. On rare nights after dinner, quite late, he shows it to them as if for the first time and at last, warily, he's decided they can be trusted. Around them, he often wears the bewildered half smile of someone frequently teased being invited to play with the bullies. The compass means something to him that they cannot understand.

"Here's the nicest thing I own," he will say in a hushed voice, as if it is a child he doesn't want to wake. "It belonged to my father."

Bea wishes he would look back at her, just once, the way he looks at the compass. When he allows her to hold it, she cups it gently in her hands. The compass is clunky and brass. The arrow reorients inside the many-pointed star. Bea never met her grandfather; he doesn't occur to her, she has nothing to miss. He died not long after her grandmother, following years of caretaking when his wife thought him a stranger, both younger than Bea's father is now.

Before he tucks the compass away, he polishes its face of her fingerprints.

*

The compass has never left his study, and they have never gone on a picnic. It is hard for Bea to imagine. Will they recline on a blanket? Will he take off his shoes?

Once they are assembled in the kitchen, bleary and disoriented—it is a weekday, he does not permit them missing school—their father starts out the door.

"A picnic?" Ulrika asks slowly. "Won't we want food, then?"

He waits on the porch as she packs hard-boiled eggs, brown bread, cold chicken, jars of milk, and a sack of sunflower seeds.

When he tries to board their rowboat with its belly full of rain, Ulrika stops him and bilges with the tin cup.

Even at the dock, the waves are white capped. It is cold for spring, the air hung with mist. He fumbles the oarlocks. His strokes are choppy and shallow. Bea is splashed in the bow.

"Aren't we headed to Bluff Cove?" asks Ulrika. But already they have cleared the moorings and arced wide of the sheltering shore, salt spray blurring their father's glasses. When he rests the oars, the current carries the boat sideways.

He takes off the compass and passes it to Bea.

"The arrow should point between the N and the W," he says, showing her. "Tell me if it doesn't. Can you do that?"

She wears the cold chain necklace, so the compass won't fall in unless she goes with it.

"The Blue Maiden?" asks Ulrika.

He squints into the wind.

Villagers note the shifting presentation of the nearby island as they do the changing face of the moon.

When a bank of fog clings to its shores, the Blue Maiden appears to float atop the water. Then the older boys in Bea's class say, "She's lifting her skirts." And when it looks like rain, "She doesn't want them soaked."

Most often, it is solidly blue, but as the color of the waves morph with the weather the island's appearance does also. It shifts from green to gray or on the clearest mornings reveals its gradations: white beach, pink granite, pine.

But when Bea thinks of the island, it is only ever blue.

She has never been there. It is not a place the villagers often go. But she knows, up close, its landscape will be powdered in a deep blue, settled on the shores like ash or the dust in a room she is not allowed to enter. Walking into its woods, she will leave a trail of footprints.

Legend says the Blue Maiden has a parallel realm, a hidden world familiar but distorted like the homes and faces in nightmares. Blockula's fields are unending, and her labyrinth, and the great halls of her lone house where witches communed with the Devil. Sailors who say the name Blockula are sure to drown, the figureheads from the prows of sunken ships in Berggrund Island's bay both proof and warning.

But Blockula isn't real, Bea reassures herself. *And if it were, boats cannot row you there. Fathers cannot take you.*

She disbelieves, too, that he can take them to the Blue Maiden. The small, uninhabited island is guarded by an underwater seawall. Its landscape, the villagers say, is the least welcoming of anyplace on God's earth. No wonder the tale of Blockula was borne from such a wasteland. They could not live on the Blue Maiden if they wanted to. The fields are dense with impassable brambles, the trees stunted and stooped by hostile winds. Visitors will be tempted to return home with a stone from the island's beaches, and then its curse will erode the thief's soul bit by bit, like winter waves eating away at Berggrund Island's bluffs. When Bea recalls the words *bit by bit* they transmute to *bite by bite*.

After an hour of heaving waves—the seat of her dress soaking through, her eyes on the quivering needle—they reach an island that is perfectly ordinary. It is so regular and real that she wonders if somehow she did not watch the compass carefully. There is no underwater seawall, nothing of the great stone gates rising beneath them, jagged and impassable as the fortress of a castle.

Instead, her father noses the boat around boulders, parting mustard-colored seaweed. The Blue Maiden looks like their own island during a drought. Dead grass, scrub brush. The only real difference is the stones covering the beach, which on Berggrund are black or gray or tan, irregularly shaped, and perfect for skipping. Here they are white, weathered smooth, and round.

"Don't get out of the boat," he says as they glide in.

He hauls them onto shore, wincing and rubbing his shoulder, rocks scraping the hull. "And don't let the tide take you. I'll be back soon."

"Where are you going?" Bea asks.

"To find a spot."

"I'm hungry," says Bea.

Tumbled by the outgoing waves, the stones sound like thunder.

Bea expects Ulrika to clamber from the boat the moment he is out of view. Instead, her sister opens the bag of food. Bea peels thin strips of skin from her apple while Ulrika cracks the hard-boiled eggs, removing their shells fragment by tiny fragment.

When Bea touches her mother's stone in her pocket—she does so often, unthinkingly—she has the fleeting impulse to toss it to shore. Every other stone there looks the same as hers, perfectly round and white, and a roiling panic starts to rise like an oncoming wave, like the time she looked too long at her feet tucked neatly under the church pew, in the row of children wearing the same shoes, pair after pair, and lost the sense that her feet belonged to her, though she was attached to them, her vision turning swimmy and bright.

She imagines her mother walking the beach, stooping to pick up the stone, sure of her steady good luck.

A howl rises from the woods.

It is no coyote. It is nothing Bea has heard before, ragged and long and mournful, and with a shiver she wonders if perhaps her father is its source.

He staggers from the woods. Something flails in his arms.

"It's Helmi," Ulrika says.

"It's not," says Bea. She says this again as her father loads the dog into the boat, as he repeats her name: "Helmi, good girl, Helmi, that's our good girl." He says to Ulrika, "Hold her, please," though the dog bares its teeth and pink gums. "Be careful. She bit me."

"That isn't Helmi," Bea says as Ulrika wraps the dog in a blanket and then in her arms. Their father takes up the oars and pushes off. Already, a bruise forms on his knuckle, the skin broken though not bleeding.

"I need you to hold her tightly," he says. "She might try to jump."

"Who's a good girl," says Ulrika as the dog crams its snout into her pocket, wolfing down the last half-peeled egg stashed there and trying to eat the napkin it is wrapped in.

"Comfort her," he says to Bea. "You're the one she trusts."

The dog shivers in Ulrika's lap, ears flat, fur matted. There is a length of rope around its neck. There is

61

a terrible, wafting smell. The dog twists to lick Ulrika's cheek.

"It's not Helmi," Bea says one last time, though they have stopped listening to her, because in fact it is, of course it is, it must be.

Helmi will not let anyone close enough to cut the rope from her neck. It dangles, frayed and graying, for months before unraveling on its own. Under the rope her fur is worn in a ring of raw skin. Even after it scars, it will be impossible to forget the rope, or the tree trunk she was tied to, because the hair at her neck never grows back.

In the hours after bringing her home, their father explains wincingly that someone must have taken her to the Blue Maiden, tied her to a tree, and left her to die.

This was how he found her, her ribs visible, the ground around the trunk scrabbled to mud and wet in a circle the length of her lead. He cut her free.

"Thank God," he says, his face in his hands. "Thank God it rained."

He makes them kneel on the parlor floor.

On most days, his relationship to God shows itself in shy glimpses that don't tend to involve them. The glossy green ribbon he tucks between his Bible's translucent pages, marking his spot. The meter of his footsteps pacing back and forth in prayer. In church he reveals a reverence nurtured all week behind a closed door. There, his hair is combed and the morning's tea stains hide beneath his robe. Behind the pulpit his voice is sure and loud, and he seems taller and older, though he has never been able to grow a beard and his hair is still brown. Back home, he sometimes stutters, and in the days after his sermons he struggles to meet their eyes.

"What happened today was a miracle," he says. It is the first of three times in Bea's life she will see him cry. Each takes her by surprise, the second when Helmi dies quietly in her sleep, the third on the night of Bea's wedding.

"How did you know where to look?" Bea asks.

"A miracle," repeats Ulrika, her eyes flat and gray.

"God told you?"

"I thought the voice that woke me this morning was your mother's," he says. "But of course, you're right." He laces his fingers tightly together.

"But why was she there?" asks Ulrika. "Who would do that?"

"I don't know." Beneath them, the floorboards creak as he begins to rock, lips moving in silent prayer. "The Devil is in this town," he says. "That's all I know."

When Bea pats Helmi, it takes a moment to recognize the sound that rises as a growl. Mysterious lumps hide in the downy undercoat of her fur. Ulrika assures Bea they are mats, but Helmi will not let them comb her. Bea thinks of her sister's efforts to untangle their own snarls, most often the culprit nothing more than a bit of fluff hidden at the knot's center.

If Helmi is not quite the same dog after her return from the Blue Maiden, then perhaps the father who has them kneel in the kitchen until Bea's kneecaps bruise is not quite the same father. And maybe Ulrika is a slightly different Ulrika, and Bea herself is changed in ways she cannot yet see.

◊

Her mother's coat yokes Bea's shoulders. Its green lining is cold against her skin. The hem trails behind her like a veil. In the mirror, its shape bells in a woman's silhouette, with Bea hidden inside it. Squinting, she can almost imagine herself older, the coat cut to her body's shape.

It makes a slippery sound as it drags down the stairs, collecting hair and dirt and dust. Ulrika waits, crouched on the landing. Bea can see the long curve of her sister's spine through the thin, flowered fabric of her dress. When she climbs onto Ulrika's shoulders, the coat's skirts drape over her sister's face. "Can you breathe?" Bea whispers as Ulrika does up the buttons, leaving one undone, a gap to look through. When they rise together, the coat falls past Ulrika's knees, as she promised it would. They are nearly as tall as the ceiling.

Bea raises the hood. It hangs low, so all she can see is the floor in front of her. They wait for him in the hallway.

Hidden in the hood's green, Bea feels her mouth tighten, her eyes turning wild in their sockets. She becomes the creature their father will meet, and she scares herself.

"You'll never believe how many herons I counted this morning," he calls, rounding the corner from the kitchen. "Eleven, on the beach. Imagine."

Even if Bea wanted to, it is too late to stop.

They lurch forward. She raises her arms as they practiced, fingers outstretched like claws. She makes a rasping sound.

When he drops his mug, the handle breaks off. From inside the hood, she can't see his face. Ulrika's shoulders shake beneath Bea's thighs, and Bea knows her sister is laughing.

"Put me down," she tells Ulrika as he sops up tea with the napkin that was tucked into his collar. Somehow, she feels Ulrika has played a trick on them both.

They have teased him before, in what small ways they can. And mostly, he seems too tired or preoccupied to care, as if sharing their giddy company is an unexpected coincidence he must wait out. When he does scold them, he calls them by their seven names: Ulrika Angelique Signe Linnea Birgitta Katarina Silasdotter and Beata Angelique Sophia Dorothea Karolina Adellisa Silasdotter.

Lined up, the names sound to Bea more like prayer than scolding.

Now he says nothing.

"Put me down," Bea demands again.

Instead, Ulrika's hand emerges from the gap she watches through to undo the rest of the coat's buttons. She ducks them out the doorway, the top of Bea's head just missing the frame. Bea grips tight to her sister's hair, curls frizzy and hot from hiding. Ulrika hurries them down the drive and around the bend on her long legs, the coat flapping.

"Look," Ulrika says, pointing to the Blue Maiden, hovering inside fog. "Blockula is lifting her skirt."

Bea clamps a firm hand over her sister's mouth.

In one swift motion, she is catapulted from Ulrika's shoulders.

Gravel is embedded in Bea's palms. The coat is streaked with mud. She refuses to cry.

"Don't say that name," Bea pants.

"Blockula. Blockula. Blockula. No one is listening."

But of course, the island itself will hear its second name and stir.

Bea gathers up the coat. Her right hand is bleeding, and her stockings are torn. She has never run so fast. Her knees and wrists throb. She veers off the road, cutting through lawns, garden beds crawling with slugs, bristling hedges, the orchard with its dew-pearled strands of web strung from tree to tree, but when she finally looks back Ulrika is nowhere in sight.

◊

"Love not the world," reads their father from the pulpit. "Neither the things that are in the world." He looks up from his Bible. "For if any man love the world, the love of the Father is not in him."

At sunset, the church's white walls turn pink as the inside of a shell.

"If we are honest with ourselves," he says, "don't we see the world for what it is? A wilderness. Full of vanity and cruelty, lust and greed."

He stands, palms open, and Bea feels wilderness infiltrating the church and surrounding him, like the climbing vine that winds up their porch steps, tendrils curling through the rotten wood at the window frame.

"We are fools, pouring our best love into this fickle place, its people. We drain ourselves." His forehead glints. "Our best love," he says again. "We can't trust this world to return it."

He closes his eyes, and silence stretches too long, as if he has fallen asleep on his feet. But then he says, "Let Spirit triumph over flesh," his voice thick. "Let us pour our love into God. Let this love fill up your heart until all worldly love is crowded out." For a moment, Bea thinks he looks down at her, but he is looking beyond her, over the congregation. "We might endeavor to love Him perfectly," he says. "As we try and fail to love each other, time and time again, with patience, gentleness, obedience, and self-control. I promise, for your efforts, He will love you back as only God can and with such perfection."

She has long been told of God's constant, monitoring presence, assured He is as real as her father, and that He disciplines only as fathers do, to strengthen faith. Those seasons when crops are infested with beetles, she understands the farmers are to blame for something riddled and rotten inside them, unrepented. Though she acts carelessly, like a heathen child—what her father calls her as he licks his thumb to clean a smudge of dirt from her forehead—she still memorizes catechism and prays throughout the day, at least when her father is watching. Yet her prayers are not so different from any other tedious but necessary ritual: braiding her hair, picking her teeth, practicing letters in her primer. A routine that never amounted to true faith, not really, but she hadn't realized the difference.

No, she has not believed in God enough to love or fear Him—or the Devil either. The immediate is always more pressing: the doctor's bag, rotten stumps, sheep with bellies full of wool, empty armoires. But for a moment, in the pink light, she believes absolutely—that God speaks directly in her father's ear, gifting picnics as miracles in exchange for love, and that the Devil sweeps through their village, possessing certain people, who in their weakness turn so wicked they would steal a dog and tie her to a tree to die. Curses are real, and the witch outside the window, and Blockula, its lone house and its labyrinth, all of it. A shiver moves across Bea's scalp.

*

69

Back home, she takes her mother's stone from her pocket. In truth, she knew from the moment she saw the white, winding beaches of the Blue Maiden that the stone belonged there, but she didn't want to be rid of it. The Devil was in her ear. Now she might throw the stone into their well or tuck it under her mattress or slide it into Samuel Axelsson's satchel as punishment for flicking Ulrika's crumpled ear, but the stone's curse doesn't work that way. It is not undone so easily. She kneels in the garden, the ground covered with mulch, and though it doesn't work this way either she digs up to her elbow in the freshly thawed earth.

"Ulrika Angelique Signe Linnea Birgitta Katarina," she whispers as she buries it, the most powerful words she knows. "Beata Angelique Sophia Dorothea Karolina Adellisa."

Part III

On the mainland, unsavory elements lurk around each corner. Their father reminds them as they disembark the ferryboat.

"What does he mean?" Bea whispers.

"Chaos," answers Ulrika.

Horses crawl with flies. Dozens of rainbows hang in the millstream's mist. The paperboy gestures wildly with ink-stained hands.

Her father's eyes are wide and pink rimmed, sweeping back and forth.

The mainland is only an hour's sail away from Berggrund on a calm day, but it feels much farther removed. They make the trip twice per year, loading up on provisions.

Bea searches each face for someone familiar.

Her father has told them little of her mother's life before the island. The scant details he does offer drain his color like a bloodletting. Their maternal grandfather was one such unsavory type who was prone to bouts of drinking and passed when Angelique was a baby. Their maternal grandmother, a prayerful but feeble woman, died of fever during her summer stay with Angelique on Berggrund.

After that summer, the islanders agreed they did not care for strangers on holiday. The inn, open for a single season, shuttered. Because Bea and Ulrika have an outsider mother, they share an aura of otherness, too—not quite true islanders, not quite newcomers.

Now the ferry makes its passage monthly or sometimes once a season. Their only visitors are shipwrecks and occasional fishing and freight boats. Sailors haul nets of flapping herring to be salted. Cattle, sheep, and horses are led in tentative single file down the plank.

Bea senses her mother's people could be anywhere among the strangers, if only she could recognize them.

She trails a woman with long red hair through the jostling crowd, not realizing until she loses her that she is lost, too. A stubborn part of her is certain if she walks just a little farther she will find her mother's girlhood garden in full flower.

Ulrika's whistle pierces the air.

Bea drags herself back toward the sound.

Huddled on the street corner, her father looks too small for his suit, gripping tight to his overflowing grocery cart. Ulrika, fourteen now, stands nearly as tall.

For the rest of the trip, he will not let go of Bea's hand. She struggles to keep pace, new boots rubbing her ankles raw.

*

In the cramped changing room, Ulrika turns away from Bea to face the wall while the seamstress fits them for new clothing. Soon Ulrika will be fifteen, and after her confirmation she can put her hair up and wear black dresses that fall to her ankles, while Bea is stuck in yellow smocks. "Why, you're a head taller," the seamstress exclaims of Ulrika. She frowns at her measuring tape, cinched around Ulrika's waist. The fabric of Ulrika's old shift tugs across her shoulders and the sleeves don't meet her wrists. Sometime over the winter—hidden by the drape of her cloak and the loosely tied apron—Ulrika's body has assumed the curved shape of their mother's coat, though the coat itself she's long outgrown. Bea has changed so little since last year that she'll only have one new dress.

At the candy shop, their father allows them each a licorice twist, their twice-yearly ritual. Instead, Bea chooses a paper carton packed tight with currants, just like the one in their kitchen.

"Look here," says the white-whiskered shopkeeper, winking at Bea as he presses a lever. A brown stub rolls across the counter and onto the floor. He waggles his pointer finger, also a stub, ending at his knuckle. "When I was your age, I stuck my finger in this cigar cutter's hole and whoop! Sliced the tip right off, just like it was a cigar. I knew the machine, too. I couldn't tell Pa why I did it."

When she was younger, the cutter would have crowded her thoughts, and before bed or on waking she would have felt the hole's cold iron rim snug as a ring around her finger and been forced to think of other things so as not to picture the falling blade.

But though last year's dress was shapeless and the new one will be also, she's learned not to let the cutter bother her, or the doctor either, or any of that. In her head she corrects him: she is quite a bit older than the shopkeeper imagines her to be.

She joins her father at the bow as they sail home, peeling currants from the solid, sticky clump. The boat cuts through froth. He tells her the pink that drained from her cheeks on the mainland has come back. Midway, tossed by waves, Ulrika is sick over the railing.

"My island daughter," he calls Bea with a smile, teeth blackened by licorice. "Imagine growing up in a place where you couldn't walk down the center of the street. Where it's not safe after dark." He pats her shoulder, as if Helmi were never taken and tied up and the name Blockula never spoken.

"You two are lucky girls," he tells her.

◊

Their classmates follow them home from school.

They are always after something. Lately, Ulrika's transformation has caught their attention.

"Giant," they shout to Ulrika. "Giant. Giant!"

"Don't look," Ulrika says when Bea risks a glance back. She spots Vera, Klaus, Katrine, Finn, Ada, and the Axelsson twins.

"Should we run?"

"We're not going anywhere," Ulrika says. "Raise your hood."

Inside it Bea feels sheltered and alone, even though she can't see what is coming up behind her.

◊

Footsteps circle the house, twigs snapping. Bea feels the unsavory element surrounding them, danger carried back from the mainland like diseased rats stowed in the packing straw. *Just our schoolmates*, she comforts herself. *A prank.*

But they've never come to the house before.

She asks Ulrika if she should get their father, though his study door is closed. Ulrika shushes her.

"Don't come crying to me when you catch your death of fever," their father used to say each time they played in the rain until their teeth chattered. "Don't come crying to me," when Bea stepped on a stinging jellyfish while running barefoot along the sand. By now they are less wild and don't cry nearly as often. Bea is starting to know better.

Ulrika grips the fire poker.

Bea chooses the coal shovel.

She feels a surge of their old camaraderie, inklings of the make-believe world they used to get lost in.

Step by step, they leave the house behind. Walking toward her fear is like wading into thick and stagnant water.

From all directions, brush crackles in the close dark.

"I see you," Ulrika shouts, though Bea sees nothing. "I'm here! I hear you!"

When Ulrika stills, Bea raises her shovel. Flashes of movement rustle the tall grass. "I see you," Bea tries to shout, but her mouth has gone dry.

Then the footsteps are behind them.

Bea wheels around. Ulrika drops her poker, but Bea keeps the shovel raised.

Her father wrenches it from her.

He leads them back into the house.

"Something was there," she tells him, though she cannot be sure. "Someone was there."

"Everything is alright," he says. "Nothing to fear." He stands on the porch in the circle of light cast by his lantern. When he comes inside, he locks the hook-and-eye latch. "Safe and sound," he says.

Beyond Ulrika, Bea has no friends. She doesn't ride her sister's shoulders anymore. They've stopped playing orphans. They've cast no more spells. Last spring, Helmi died in her sleep beside the fire. Many days, when they get home from school, Ulrika wants to be alone. She takes long walks with the red book, leaving Bea behind.

Even their classmate Oscar, whose mother greases him with lanolin every November before sewing him into the underclothes he wears through April, is tolerated by the other children so long as he keeps his smell at some distance, sprawling nearby in the yellowed schoolyard grass. This kind of trespass is something Bea doesn't try.

By now, she suspects that she and Ulrika are irredeemably ugly.

When she was younger, she felt radiant, leaping surefooted from rock to rock. Colors darted inside her like fish under the surface of the shallows, shimmering pink or gold or green.

Now when others look at her, she is aware that her plain little face stares dimly back.

Her eyes are mismatched colors, and she's as small for her age as Ulrika is large. By the end of summer, freckles crowd her mouth. She slips through the classroom unnoticed. At home, she's taken to clearing her throat when she enters the room. Inevitably, the sound startles her father or Ulrika, who did not see her come in. She knows when she is invisible because the air is charged and the hairs on her arms stand on end.

Bea struggles to see Ulrika as anything but beautiful. But she's beginning to understand this is merely an illusion caused by love. There is a white-blond starburst of hair between her sister's eyebrows, her front teeth overlap, her curls are uncombed, and her hands are large and chapped. Lars Lund brings stilts to school made of paint cans and rope, tottering around the yard, yelling, "Who am I?" while eyeing Ulrika. The topsoil scrapes easily to bedrock, so each metal step rasps. Day after day, the older boys challenge Ulrika to arm wrestle and she ignores them. She finally relents, slamming their fists into the desk, but when their knuckles bruise overnight they tell her she hasn't won at all, only proved a point that she is brutish.

Bit by bit, Bea is beginning to believe them.

When Ulrika returns from gathering mushrooms with her cheek scratched and her dress torn and dirty, she tells Bea they challenged her to wrestle once more. "They think they're stronger," Ulrika says. "But I beat them."

◊

The only other friendless child is Elias Axelsson.

By now, he is a better reader and writer than anyone at school and can solve equations faster than his twin brothers—Samuel and Erik—who are six years older and handsome. His penmanship is delicate and looping, like a carefully tended vine. When the teacher makes Elias recite a poem, the lenses of his glasses fog at the final stanza, though he does not cry.

Afterward, Lars Lund knocks the thin, gold frames from Elias's face and steps on them as if by accident. Elias's brothers—Lars's friends—pretend it is so.

Bea eats with Elias beneath the dogwood, inside a circle of red leaves. Without his glasses, his bare face looks unfinished.

Ulrika does not join them. She leans alone against the fence.

Across the schoolyard, the boys crouch over the sunken sandpit of the antlion's den. They take turns huffing the sand away, to expose the furred beetle hidden underneath. "Caught it!" they scream, as it burrows down once more. Whoever fails to blow forcefully enough is made to touch the antlion's bristly pincers. Elias always lost, so he stopped playing long ago.

By the end of the day they will sneak the scrabbling beetle into his collar.

*

However ugly Bea becomes, she knows Elias is uglier. She cannot stop herself from cataloguing precisely why.

His forehead is high with a widow's peak. His ears sit too low on his head, hidden beneath his curls. His eyes are large, wet, and wide set, with lashes like those on the grassland's calves. He has an upturned nose with a tiny cleft at its tip that mirrors the cleft on his chin. Once she told him about the matching clefts, and he blushed as if pleased.

Year after year, he's continued wearing a version of the same velvet overcoat, fine shirts and trousers beneath. He used to remove the coat to swim, until their schoolmates stole it from the stream bank, throwing it high into the branches of a fir tree. Then he stopped swimming. A locket hangs around his neck in the shape of a book, blue pills inside it.

He catches her looking and stares back.

When others refer to what exists between Bea and Elias as friendship, both protest. But each lunchtime, he shows her trinkets collected from his sprawling house.

Now he empties his pockets. He passes her five thimbles to dress her fingertips. The long-rooted tooth of a sow. A tiny boat trapped inside a tiny bottle. A rowan branch, whittled to a thin animal shape. She can make out paws tucked against its body, haunches, flattened ears, and pointed snout.

She runs a finger down the smooth length of its back, closing her fist around it. It gives her the good feeling of holding the Blue Maiden stone. She wants for it terribly, as if a fissure has split her center and is quickly turning into a chasm.

"What is it?"

"A protector."

"I'll trade you," says Bea.

"I need it," Elias says.

But the carving has a hold on her.

"I can bring jewelry," she promises, glancing at Ulrika, who does not look back. Elias shakes his head. "A pendant with the profile of a beautiful woman," she whispers. "A silver ring." She scans the inventory of her life for its finest things.

"I have a compass," she blurts out. "In a velvet-lined box."

A bad feeling builds inside her. She invites Elias to seesaw. The wind catches their hair, bells her skirt. When the teacher calls them in, Elias is midair, and she leaps off to send him thunking to the ground.

"Can't I come with you?" Bea asks when Ulrika leaves to forage fresh herbs for dinner.

"No."

"Are you angry? Did you overhear me?" Bea almost hopes she did, to be noticed.

"Nothing like that."

"Please," says Bea, taking up her own basket.

"You'll only slow me down."

All summer and fall Ulrika has canned and pickled, making jam from lingonberries and bilberries and the firm, sour strawberries in their front field that hardly ripen. She harvests stinging nettle that sweetens in potato soup and dandelion petals to steep in Bea's lemonade, recipes from the red book. Her fingernails are dirty, her cuticles raw. Mornings and evenings the kitchen fills with Ulrika's humming and steam that fogs the windows.

Bea tells herself she is merely going for her own walk. She dawdles through back pastures, stepping around cow pats. The wind whips her braids and scarf, rustling the leaves, their crisp-edged color like flames. When she nears the woods, she spots her sister crouched in the distance. Bea drops, crawling through the sharp undergrowth, and Ulrika stills, her eyes searching the trees around her. Then she bellows, "Leave me alone!"

"It's only me," Bea wants to announce. But she stays belly down, frozen, watching.

She has never seen her sister furious, yanking up plants by their feathered leaves, shaking clean the roots. Parsley. A punishment. Ulrika knows Bea will pick out each limp, green fleck from her dinner and wipe it on the underside of the table. Ulrika ties the bunches off with a length of red string. The basket overflows.

For the first time, Bea is glad to be small and invisible.

She trails Ulrika to the village center, ducking behind shrubs and stone walls, all the way to the house where Lars lives. In the fading light, Ulrika hurries to the porch and drops a bundle of parsley on the doorstep.

Bea steps out from a copse of oak. "Caught you," she says.

It is so rare that her sister looks dismayed. She looks like she will cry.

Twisting Bea's wrist, she drags her to the end of the drive.

"What are you doing?"

"They're gifts," Ulrika mutters, and Bea is afraid she really will cry, that Bea has made her do so for the first time. She feels a flicker of pride. "For our schoolmates," Ulrika says. "I wanted to drop them in secret."

"Why?"

"That's the best kind of present."

"Do you fancy Lars?"

"It's late," Ulrika says. "It was a silly idea."

"Let's just finish," says Bea. "They'll wilt." She takes two bunches from the basket.

"Wait," Ulrika says, rolling her eyes. "Don't waste any by eating it. And keep your scarf and gloves on. You don't want to catch cold."

"I'm not a baby," Bea says.

But later, because she is not supposed to, she sneaks a nibble, though it smells of the mold that speckles their walls in summer, and it wicks the spit from her tongue. She chews until it goes dry in the pocket of her cheek, like cud.

There are not enough bouquets for everyone, so Ulrika picks where to go next, house by house. They take the porch steps lightly, pausing when the wood creaks. At Elias's, Bea holds her hand over her mouth, afraid a laugh like a bark will sound from her, and once it starts it won't stop.

"Run," Ulrika whispers when the bouquet is dropped, and Bea sprints with her back stooped, imagining they are chased. It is their father's hand she envisions clamping down on her, as if each house belongs to him, and then they are safe, collapsed behind the hedge, and she is giggling and queasy with gift giving.

86

On one of the parsleys there is a spray of white flowers, delicate as Queen Anne's lace. She picks the sprig and splits it, tucking the stem behind her ear.

"I told you not to touch that," Ulrika says, swatting the bloom from Bea's hair.

"It was bolted," she says. "It would have been bitter." She tucks the other stem through Ulrika's buttonhole, as if her sister were a boy on his way to a dance.

They deliver the bitter bouquet to Ada, who steals Bea's chalk and grinds it into dust, and the last bedraggled bunch to Klaus, pigs with untrimmed hooves hobbling in his front yard.

"How did it get so late?" Bea hears herself asking, again and again, as they walk home in the dark, though she is not sure, really, what time it could be.

Sweat beads on her upper lip. The moon is a crescent.

She has the strange sensation that she might be sleep-walking, as if any moment Ulrika will slowly turn to her and ask her for her name.

As she lies on her back under the quilt, the shimmery promise of all the gifts waiting in the dark across town keeps her awake, and her lips begin to tingle, and her tongue begins to burn, and spit floods her mouth. Each time she swallows, it fills swiftly up again.

The hallway pitches like a ship's deck. She knocks a frame from the wall, needlepoint of her father's favorite psalm. The stairs to Ulrika are impossible to climb.

"Beata," scolds her father when she comes crawling into his study.

She opens her mouth and drool pours out.

"I got sick," she wants to explain, but the sound is slurred and soft. She wishes she could tell him, "I'm awake," but her tongue is heavy.

He kneels beside her. *To pray*, she thinks, but his eyes meet hers instead of closing, and he holds her gaze steadily for perhaps the first time in her life, his expression startling in its tenderness and concern. It is a look she has seen—as he polished his compass or smoothed Helmi's fur before she stopped letting him pat her—but it has never been directed toward Bea with such intensity. She feels certain, even as her limbs begin to tingle and then to numb, that she is almost painfully dear to him.

She will recall how he looks at her on this night over and over, and once will even try to describe it to him as his face is cold and hard but will fumble and go quiet. Perhaps what the look suggests can never be mentioned, and it's the kind of thing that only exists between them once.

But now, just for a moment, it seems his true face is unmasked, as if long before she existed this was simply how he took in the world around him and the people in it.

"Your pupils are tiny," he says with gentle wonder. "What did you do?"

And then a warm, thin stream runs down her thigh. His face snaps back to itself. "What did you do?" he repeats, words sharp, sweeping her up into his arms.

Tonight, the church seems to be a living thing, its domed ceiling a body's cavern, the walls animate and breathing. Bea feels witnessed, if not by God then by the sentient space, the gold-lit limestone.

"God has gifted us a miracle," her father announces from the pulpit in the sure-spoken voice he uses for sermons, so different from his own. His eyes search, then land on Bea.

For six days, they've gone unpunished for the dangerous gifts they delivered—not one spanking, not even a lecture. To Bea, this is the miracle.

There have been no deaths or illnesses to speak of beyond her own.

Even now, she questions her lingering memories—drooping bouquets, white sprig at her sister's lapel. Perhaps she really was playing where she shouldn't have been, just as Ulrika said, and didn't heed the warning.

◊

Six nights ago, the doctor fed her cloying syrup. He tipped her to her side to wretch, and Ulrika explained she'd found Bea playing near a patch of poison hemlock. Though

Ulrika appeared calm as always, she radiated vibratory energy—perhaps she always did, and Bea was just now noticing—like a hovering dragonfly surrounded by the blur of its wings.

"But I made sure she hadn't touched it," Ulrika said softly. "I don't know why she'd eat it."

"Hemlock?" the doctor asked. "You're certain?"

Ulrika nodded.

"Careless," said their father, voice cracking. "You'll be to blame, when she dies."

"Pastor," the doctor interrupted. "Forgive me. She's only a girl."

Later, Ulrika returned breathlessly with Bruna.

Ulrika panted in Bea's ear, "I ran as fast as I could. I couldn't run any faster."

"What's she doing here?" said their father. "You're not needed."

"Silas," answered Bruna, holding up her hand. "Please." Her long white hair draped against Bea like a curtain. She poured bitter liquid down Bea's throat. "Just a little acorn broth," she said, wiping Bea's mouth as she choked. "Now swallow this nice strong coffee." Bea imagined the sacred white snake alive in Bruna's stomach, coiled to strike, but was too weak to feel afraid. Bruna offered no further remedy except to hold Bea's hand, her palm warm and dry and soft. "Oh, you girls," she whispered. "So much like your mother. I'm always here if you need me. I am a friend."

In those early hours, Bea thought of the bouquets of leaves—not parsley after all but poison—waiting on their neighbors' doorsteps, bubbling in their stews, or wilting in their kitchens. Each day, Ulrika studied the red book, and so she must have known the difference. If Bea's tongue worked properly and she could summon energy to speak, she would have said to Ulrika, "Confess. Warn them." Instead, she stared at Ulrika and Ulrika stared back, giving the subtlest shake of her head, as if reading Bea's thoughts.

Bea didn't float above herself looking down, as she'd heard happened when you died. But her spirit settled just beyond the boundary of her skin, like a leaf drifting on the surface of water.

Two days after eating hemlock, Bea suspected she could talk but chose to keep quiet. And when she could move her limbs again, she wanted to lie still a little longer. Ulrika brought no news, only ice dollies she pressed to Bea's brow. The ice was the dolly's head and her skirt the dishcloth it was wrapped in, synched with string, smelling of Ulrika's dresses—kitchen grease and smoke. When the head melted the skirt got drenched.

"I have something you need," Ulrika said, climbing into Bea's bed, tucking Elias's animal carving into Bea's palm. Bea's fist closed around it. "Make her better. Please, make her better."

"What did you trade?" Bea asked, body rigid and unused voice raspy.

91

"You're back," Ulrika said. "Thank God, you're back."

"What did you trade?"

Ulrika wiped her eyes.

"What if I gave him Father's precious compass, after all?" she said, hitching the corner of her mouth into the slightest smile.

This got Bea out of bed, the carving falling to the floor.

"Beata. I'm teasing."

Bea reached the hallway on shaking legs, Ulrika calling, "You know I wouldn't. I only said it because you did."

The door to their father's study was open. "You're feeling better," he said, rising. He held her, too tightly. "Where's your sister?"

"Show me the compass?" asked Bea.

"Are you feverish?" He guided her to his chair, warm from him. "You're drained of color."

"Please," she begged. She found it difficult to breathe until he slid open the drawer, creaked open the box, and there was the compass, nestled in its velvet.

"I have something to tell you," Bea said.

The following day, she was well enough to return to school.

Ulrika bundled her as she'd done when they were little, Bea stiff limbed under many layers. It seemed, in just two days' time, her muscles had softened. The glare of sun on water made her squint. The world glimmered. Today, the Blue Maiden was in clear view, white stone beach and green scrub. She pulled up her hood. Everything beyond her bedroom walls had carried on relentlessly.

When their classmates caught up to them, Vera darted ahead.

"Whore," she said, the word too round and soft for what it meant, lobbed at them like an overripe fruit.

"Don't listen," said Ulrika.

"Whoring witch," purred a voice from behind her. "Just like your mother."

The voice belonged to Klaus, who blocked their path. He stood eye to eye with Ulrika, looking her up and down as the others circled. "When I lifted your skirt, all I found between your legs was a blood-crazed bat."

"That's not what I felt," Lars said. "I felt a hairy black spider."

"Let us go," said Ulrika. She reached into her coat and pulled out the boning knife.

◊

Now Bea holds her breath, and the church breathes for her.

"Not one week ago, a poison was delivered to your doorsteps," says her father. At once, it seems her blood flows out the soles of her feet. "Yet here you all are, unharmed. How is it so?"

When Bea confessed about the gifts he'd patted her hair with a heavy hand and said only, "Good you told me," and for three days had not spoken of it, and she believed they were absolved.

"Each day, all day, my whole life long, I pray," he says. "I ask, seek, knock, and beg, faithful that answers, blessings, God's mercy will be mine. I keep knocking, until my knuckles bleed, because God is a perfect father. Even the most negligent parent among us, so the scripture says, would not serve his child a snake when they hungered for fish. Would not give his neighbor a scorpion when they came for an egg. So why would God, blessed Father, deliver us anything but nourishment and care?

"It was God who kept this village safe. This, the loving blessing we pray for each day, antidote to any poison. We give thanks."

They kneel. Ulrika grips Bea's hand, her fingers digging in.

"Recall," he continues, "what Jesus bestows upon his followers: Authority to tread on serpents and scorpions, and over all the power of the Enemy. A promise of protection. Dear neighbors, what landed at your doors was no less poison than scorpion or snake. We know well who delivers such gifts. Satan himself, and those who do the bidding of a false father. A murderer. A father of lies.

"Stay vigilant. Ask: Which father do I serve today? Whose voice answers when I call? Is it truly God our Father? Are you sure?"

Behind Bea there is a hiss. She looks back to see Elias reading from the red book—flash of color among splayed Bibles—and his mother twisting his ear as she snatches the book away.

So this was the trade. The most precious thing Ulrika could offer.

Bea has not touched the carving since Ulrika brought it to her bedside.

Their father stares down at his hands, two closed fists. "Sometimes I envy our ancestors' conviction," he says softly, "in the Devil they could see. An age of hysteria, yes. But they knew exactly what he looked like. Where he lived. To be so sure of guilt versus innocence! Of pacts written in blood!

"The enlightened among us know the Devil takes no human form. Only Christ the Son could. But make no mistake, he is no less real or ruthless. He is violent. Waiting to devour us. Drawn not only to disbelief but also to our strongest faith. He wants torment, anguish, shame. Wants us certain we've sinned so terribly God cannot reach us."

His knuckles rap the pulpit. "It isn't so. It isn't so. Return. Repent. And the red of your sins will be white as wool."

In the silence, Ada's mother rises. "Your girls dropped the poison at my door, did they not? I saw them run. Is God, then, the master of your house?"

His gaze lands on them, startling, staring. Bea is braced for anger. What she sees is fear.

As if a spell has broken, he seems to shrink in size. "It's true." His voice is his own again, shoulders slumped and cheeks flushed. "Poison hemlock. On that day, they were no daughters of God." He crosses himself. "But they were daughters of mine. Who I allowed to run wild. And I am truly sorry."

"Are they?"

"I'll make sure of it." He shakes his head. "I prayed so long for a wife. Children. But which father answered those prayers? Maybe all along I've had two snakes, curled in the beds in my very house. I wasn't vigilant. I grew fond of them. I don't know. I don't know."

He removes his glasses, cleaning them slowly on his sleeve.

"Would you be so generous as to pray for me," he says. "I am feeling a bit ill. Let us pray also for the souls of my girls."

He orders them down into the dank, earthy chill of the root cellar.

When Ulrika cooks, she often sends Bea to the cellar for ingredients. The low ceiling, strung with spider webs, forces Ulrika to stoop.

What doesn't trouble Bea in daylight—daddy long-legs creeping up her sleeves in the garden—makes her flail underground, a tickling real or imagined at the back of the neck. Once, she reached her hand into the candlelit barrel of onions and found them crawling with mice. The holes in the floorboards patched, she still snatches up potatoes, squash, and cabbage quickly from their barrels, afraid to look too closely. The cellar's trapdoor is crosshatched with claw marks, as if an animal scrabbled to get out. There are sides of cured meat hanging from the ceiling on silver hooks, even worse when the hooks are empty. And there are rows upon rows of jars—pickled pigs' feet, dreaded green beans, open-eyed and frowning smelt.

The back shelves are lined with preserves that have been there as long as she can remember, lids furry with dust and some of them bloated, their contents turned unidentifiable though Ulrika refuses to dump them out. It is

Ulrika's job stocking the root cellar, though Bea helps to core rot from strawberries or spear plums with a skewer so they drink up syrup, because soon it will be her job, too.

Their father's punishments have always been rare, nothing like the schoolhouse paddlings. Once or twice, she has been spanked. Only on occasion denied food or drink.

What from the outside might seem like punishment Bea knows mainly as absentmindedness—when Ulrika was sick and Bea very young, how he filled her bath with boiling water, insisted it must have cooled, was getting cold. She dipped her foot in then drew it out, bright red to the ankle. She climbed into the steaming tub anyway and tried to stand it.

Even as he closes the door and slides the latch, and Ulrika's voice in the dark says, "He's locking us in," she still thinks this must be absentmindedness.

His footsteps cross the kitchen, and she calls to him.

What light leaks through the cracks between floorboards is not enough to see her own hands, stretched out in search of the ladder. All she has to do is climb it and pound on the underside of the door, and she knows it will open to the kitchen's warmth, and he will be baffled that in hunger and distraction and the distress of the morning he sent them down to collect what was needed for their usual Sunday supper, and then, momentarily, forgot them.

"He's coming back," Bea says, still fumbling for the ladder, triumphant and relieved. Above them, something drags across the kitchen floor. "We're down here!" she yells.

The heaviness heaves to a stop.

"He's blocked the door," says Ulrika.

Each time Ulrika speaks, her voice seems to come from a different direction, close and then distant, as if the cellar expands and contracts. "I almost killed you," she says, when Bea asks how she could possibly trade the red book to Elias. "I can't be trusted. If you lived, I swore I'd never read it again."

"Stop pacing."

"I'm not," Ulrika says, close by this time. "I'm right here."

Bea searches for Ulrika's outline, as the forms looming in her room after she turns down the lamp eventually announce themselves: coat rack, mirror, armoire, those tall, thin shapes standing over her nothing but the bed's four posts.

All she sees is bright color, like when she presses on her closed eyelids or stirs up phosphorescence from the black bay, lying with Ulrika on the pier's slick edge.

Hours pass.

"They attacked me," says a small voice. Ulrika's but not Ulrika's. Fainter. Younger. "In the reeds. Lars and Klaus, Erik or Samuel, or both. It was hard to tell who. The girls kept lookout."

Bea is afraid. She says nothing. When she stays quiet long enough, it is as if the voice never spoke at all. And in the silence, Bea has the prickling awareness that she's entirely alone in the cellar's dark. Or worse, that her companion is not Ulrika, but a feral and menacing shadow, summoned, surrounding her.

When she stretches out her arms she grabs at empty air.

"Where are you?" she whimpers, to no reply. "Where are you?" Something brushes her coat and she thrashes. "Who are you?" She doesn't realize she is screaming until there is weight on top of her, holding her down, and it is hard to catch her breath. A voice repeats, "Beata, Beata, it's me, it's me, it's me."

"You're not my sister," she says, struggling, stilling, rocked calm.

"Ulrika?" she asks finally.

"Bea," answers Ulrika.

"I'm sorry," she says. "I'm very hungry."

"Me too."

Then she's alone again.

A jar pops open. She hears the close, soft sound of chewing and smells Ulrika's sugary breath. Her mouth begins to water as the cold glass is passed over.

They are only allowed plums on rare Sundays when the bishop visits, and Christmas Eve. Such decadent sweetness is to be savored, served on a special ivory dish, their skins coloring the syrup they soak in. On average days, Bea is permitted a single spoonful of jam or currants in her oatmeal.

They will eat beyond the point of hunger: small, whole fish with delicate bones that crunch as they chew; cabbage that reeks of her stockings when they stiffen after months of wear; in the jar with a dusted lid something disintegrated, like rain-damp soil. *Beets*, she realizes but doesn't say, a gift to name what Ulrika cannot. When her belly aches and she is cold and Ulrika lies down to sleep, time slips from her again. She thinks of her sister's continuous efforts to stock the cellar, and the poison she allowed Bea to eat and to deliver, and the punishment Ulrika deserves but not Bea, not really. She was tricked. She confessed.

She will feel her way to what seems the corner, the bad feeling inside her spilling over, and without wondering what's in the rest of the jars will open every lid she can loose and dump the contents out.

But for now, she savors the plums.

When at last their father lets them out, the light makes Bea cry, though she has resolved not to. His face, slack and gray, peers down at them.

"What a waste," he says, taking in the spilled store of food, then disappearing again.

Bea closes her eyes, the afterimage of the trapdoor a red imprint.

Illuminated around her: the scattered, empty jars, the pile of slop in the corner, her sister curled up and unchanged, and the cellar, too, unchanged, though in the many hours in pitch-dark she knew not only the room's form to shift but also Ulrika's and finally her own—contorting and stretching, roving and malleable, terrifying. Again and again, she had touched the features of her face.

"What did you do?" Ulrika says, eyeing the wreckage Bea caused while Ulrika slept.

Perhaps, Bea thinks, *they will keep me in the cellar.*

For a moment this seems less punishing than opening her eyes to Ulrika's searching look. Better to be closed in the dark, the world muffled overhead, than to climb the ladder and stand exposed to pale daylight.

Her hands on the rungs are stained red. Her body aches.

He is waiting in his nightshirt, as if for once in his life he went to bed at a normal hour and slept, so has nothing to do with the mess around him, a tipped chair and broken glass, the kitchen door open to a windstorm that blows in leaves.

"Is it morning?" Bea asks. Has a whole day passed, a whole night?

"What will it take," he says, "for you to learn to behave?" His eyes cast around the kitchen and his voice shakes. "I am your father. You will obey me."

Ulrika rights the chair and guides him into it. His bare legs are thin and white.

In the washroom mirror, Bea's mouth and chin are stained the faint red of her fingers. Her church dress thuds to the floor like a caul.

Her sister does not knock. "That pantry gets us through winter," Ulrika says, filling the basin, steam rising. "Do you ever think how much work you make for me?"

Bea scrubs hard at her face.

"No," she says, dripping. "What else would you do?"

"You're a little beast," says Ulrika, handing Bea a fresh towel. "Aren't you?"

Already the table is laid for breakfast, porridge congealing, brimful cups of bitter tea, Ulrika in her crisp apron and a basket of pears waiting to be cored, as if everything were normal. Bea sneaks the knife into her pocket.

"I'm full," she says, running out into the gale. "Beata," Ulrika calls behind her. But Bea does not look back.

She leans her whole weight against the wind and is held.

From a distance, her schoolmates' laughter sounds like the squall of gulls. But when they stagger to catch up, it is only laughter.

They keep pace alongside her.

Lars leans down to say, "If it isn't the snake herself." Her hair whips his cheek. "Why did you want to poison us?" he asks. "What did we do to deserve that?"

"Plenty," Bea says.

"Witch," Vera says, so quietly Bea cannot be certain she heard correctly over the wind.

"Don't mind her," says Samuel.

"Are you like Ulrika?" Finn asks. "Can't take a little teasing?"

"I didn't know it was poison."

"Sure you didn't," Katrine says.

Bea tells them, then, how she nearly died, how she should have. For the first time they are listening, rapt. She finds herself bragging of her soul leaving her body.

"Ask the doctor if you don't believe me. Ask my father."

"Poor thing," Katrine says and seems sincere.

"Is that why you're out here alone?" asks Ada. "Outside your sister's shadow? If I were you, I'd be scared."

"I'm not scared."

"You should be," says Lars. "Not of us. Of Ulrika. She's mad."

Bea gives the smallest smile of assent. Yes, maybe her family has gone mad.

"Mad and dim," Erik says. "If she thinks we're going to eat a bunch of grubby weeds from who knows who."

"If she thinks my ma doesn't know hemlock," adds Lars. "Some miracle."

"Who can blame you," Katrine says, "for wanting to be rid of her. Ulrika treats you like a baby."

"How old are you anyway?" asks Ada.

Just like that, she is one of them.

Her whole life, Bea has taken them in while they've overlooked her. She knows Ada is fourteen, same as Ulrika, and hates celery root, and collects green marbles, can sneeze up to sixteen times straight during hay fever season, is best in the village at dancing the polska. Bea can tell the Axelsson twins apart because when Samuel smiles he has a dimple on his left cheek, while Erik's is on the right.

"You can't be a day over seven," Ada says.

"I'm eleven," Bea lies.

"Shame," says Erik. "I planned to steal a kiss at the spring dance, but if she's seven I suppose I'll wait."

"She's ten," says Samuel quietly, glancing at her. "Same age as Elias."

"Besides," Katrine says, "your brother's the one she's sweet on."

"Samuel?" says Erik, clutching his chest. Samuel's cheeks glow.

"Elias, of course," says Katrine.

Bea lets them see her shudder. "Never."

"You'll break his heart," says Samuel. "You should see the poems he writes."

Darting alongside them she is sharp, light on her feet. Finn then Erik then Lars offer her rides on their shoulders. When she declines, Lars crows, "There it is! A real smile." In the schoolyard, Ada redoes the braids Ulrika tied. "I can't believe you two are sisters," she tells Bea, yanking each section tight. "You're absolutely nothing alike."

◊

"Please," say Elias, as Lars passes out the poems.

Elias is backed against the bridge's moss-green arch, his things strewn on the bank. Ada wears his cap. Katrine gnaws his apple. Bea does nothing. She did nothing when Lars pulled the red book from Elias's satchel and flipped through, pressed flowers fluttering down, or when he held up the page with the drawing of hemlock in bloom, like the Queen Anne's lace of bridal crowns, and tore it out, and then a handful of others. The knife is in her pocket, but she merely rubs her thumb over the dull blade, and when the bag is tossed to her she rifles through it like all of them, and when the poem is offered to her she takes it.

"Samuel tells us you're quite accomplished," says Ada.

"Please don't," says Elias.

"Bea, you read first," says Lars. "I promise you'll like this one."

She is not sharp. She is smooth and worn as driftwood. The voice that comes from her is low and measured.

Caves flood, crows pick apart a mouse.

"Stop reading," Elias begs.

A girl pins up her braids, one eye blue and one eye brown.

"Stop," he says again.

She drones on, the estuary burbles, she closes her eyes. In her mind, she joins Elias on the seesaw, the tails of his coat rising and falling. She hovers midair, and then he does. There is no place to look but his face.

Elias is sent to boarding school on the mainland, the red book disappearing with him.

"A mind like his?" The teacher brushes chalk handprints from her skirt. "He should have left here years ago."

"Thinks he's too good for us," grumbles Erik.

Ada, radiant in her white sling, brags of the size of the bruise, how she heard her wrist snap, and they had to tie her down setting the bone.

"He *attacked* me," Ada says, and is fond of repeating—all spring Katrine taking Ada's dictation and Samuel hefting her books—when the truth is Elias was lunging for Bea. Ada merely lost her footing.

Why is it Bea wants to shake her by the shoulders until her crooked wrist rattles? *I'm the one he was after,* she imagines herself saying. *Me. Me.*

Now and then, Bea still walks with them. She keeps to the periphery, the smell of Oscar wafting. Alone, she runs through the woods, her arms scratched by branches. The caterpillar she sneaks into her pocket finds a hole in the seam, and during church service inches down her thigh. Though it looks harmlessly soft the tiny hairs needle, and by morning a red trail loops along her skin. She traps butterflies and lets them batter dust from their wings against her cupped palms. When she opens her hands, the insect is alive but immobile, feelers twitching. It won't fly off, even if she blows on it. She shows the trick to Oscar and calls it taming. In the grassland, she tosses herself from the rotting rowboat, crickets springing up.

The letter she bottles begins: *Dear Stranger, I am ten years old and stranded. If you find this, please help.* It disappears on the outgoing tide.

For days, Bea scans the beach, and when she finds her bottle, it's still thrilling to unfurl the tight scroll, the ink only just beginning to blur.

She lies on her belly on a broad slab of granite, covered in algae soft as fur. The tide lolls its way in. Seams of light shimmy on the waves. She closes her eyes. The estuary trickles, salt water meeting fresh. She waits for the rock to rise up under her and carry her away.

◊

In the years that follow, she is a beast.

Eleven at last, her blood arrives early and heavy. She hides the soiled cloths beneath the bed. Sweat darkens the armpits of her dresses.

Age twelve, she cannot stop herself from scratching her scalp over her desk to watch dry skin rain down, a compulsion, as is the urge to rub certain objects between her legs: hairbrush paddle, animal carving, the smooth wooden head of her doll. Friction turns the flannel of her nightgown hot. Hair grows as if conjured.

Thirteen, and her nipples ache, and her father's whistling incenses her, as does Ulrika's open-mouthed chewing, which she catalogues in her diary meal by meal, her pen nib tearing the paper.

Fourteen, spots brew beneath her skin. When Lars remarks, she lies and says they're fleabites. She cools her face and neck and back and chest with ice chips. *I will die a spinster*, she tells her journal. She keeps her head down.

Fifteen, the visions begin.

Her fear is nonsensical. A scary story she should have long ago outgrown. When she was little—the warmth of her sister alongside her—she could demand the story. Awake with the flickering lantern, changing moon, shelter of blankets, and Ulrika's breath at her ear, fear was laced with delicious comfort. "When children have been very bad," Ulrika whispered, "when they have not done their chores and neglected their prayers, the woman comes for them in a rage, contorting her face on the windowpane."

Later, on nights Bea was taut with fright, Ulrika would roll her eyes and say, "You know it's make-believe, right? A fairy tale? Witches aren't real. No one is coming."

Now Ulrika keeps her door locked.

Each evening, Bea opens the bedroom window to hold out her hand, so someone watching will see a girl with no reason to be afraid.

She sleeps with her mother's coat bunched at her back like a body. Now her mother's ring fits her finger. If she falls asleep wearing it, by morning the metal leaves behind an itchy green mark, faintly raised, like a second ring embossed on her skin.

The visions began as small harbingers.

She opened her eyes to a snake in the sheets. Leapt to her feet. Lit the lantern. Shook the blanket. She was practical, flipping pillows, inspecting each inch of her nightgown and hair.

The dreamworld was a sea she trawled with a dragnet. In the liminal gap between sleeping and waking, the figments she brought back were as real as she was.

Centipedes and tadpoles.

A starfish that moved like a spider, twirling down from the ceiling on a thin thread.

A bat, snug in the hollow of her throat.

A leech, latched to her thigh.

She slapped herself, flailed, exclaimed as if to Ulrika, "Do you see it? Can't you see it?" Pointing to the ceiling, the chimney, the window, she said, "That's where they come from, that's how they get in," her voice urgent and angry. And then coming to, she answered herself, "You're alright. Nothing there. Back to bed."

In a tree outside the window, a raccoon nibbled plums. It made wet sounds as it chewed and swallowed, its fingers deft and nimble, but no, there was no tree outside the window, no plums. The eyes glinted.

Helmi wagged her tail beside the bed. On her stomach, a second mouth snarled and gnashed.

Who can arrive next, but the woman?

The woman Bea waits for is featureless, unlike those in the story who appeared as themselves, coaxing and trusted mothers and teachers, sisters and aunts. She is pliable. She will find a way in. When she stands over Bea's bed, her figure will be off in a way difficult to name— perhaps it's her arms that are too long, or her fingers, or her neck. Perhaps her limbs' joints are not quite in their proper places, or they bend ever so slightly in the wrong direction. Bea thinks of Ada, gone pale on the estuary's slippery bank, holding up her crooked wrist, saying with surprise, "He attacked me."

To lull herself to sleep, she writes the story on the roof of her mouth with the tip of her tongue.

B-L-O-C-K-U-L-A.
         The letters tickle.

To spell the name is better than to say it, but still she clamps a hand over her mouth, then kisses her palm and imagines Samuel, who lately she's caught looking at her during lessons.

Bea does not have to journey anywhere to greet the Devil. She breathes him in and out like a puff of smoke stolen from her father's pipe. In the week before her blood comes, he plays behind her irises and at the corners of her smile, his presence in clearings, and the boil that forms on the barmaid's upper lip but never drains, and the slaughtered one-eyed cow whose meat proves too gristly to chew. He is there in the urge to drape herself in jewelry, the stubborn pleasure she still takes in plums, the strand of long white hair she pulls from the back of her throat.

And late, late at night, she is unenlightened. In those hours, the Devil of Bea's imagination takes a human form, as real as she is. Blockula is no figment, then. As if she's been there many times before, she sees it clearly: color-less landscape, house like her own but taller and thinner, rooms like their own but crooked. Outside, a meadow crawls with shadows, a labyrinth never ends. Inside, the Devil stalks the halls. But what troubles her most is the dawning sense that what happens on Blockula will happen to Bea alone, no matter how the story goes.

The lamp makes a circle of light on the ceiling. The clock's gears grind before it chimes—*one-two-three*—and the last note blends with the sound of her body's inner workings, only audible when the house grows quiet, a faint but constant ringing as if she, too, is a struck bell.

Over breakfast, the world is muffled. Neither her father nor Ulrika notice how her eyelid has begun to twitch.

Nothing seems to trouble her sister's sleep. She rises before dawn to cut bruises from potatoes, starch linens until her palms crack, bake butter cake for lanky Oscar. This, the uninvited courtship Ulrika's years of canning and baking and sweeping and stitching have added up to—a limp bouquet Ulrika hurries to revive in water, Oscar smiling from the stoop with canines the size of milk teeth as if adult ones never came in. "Count yourself lucky," their father tells Ulrika often of Oscar's affections. "A decent, levelheaded boy." At least, by now, Oscar has learned to keep clean.

Bea cuts a thick slice of cake for herself.

"Tell me again," she asks Ulrika over the kettle's hiss, "about the witching hour?"

Their father glances up, his smile like a shrug. "A time of too few prayers," he answers. "When souls are most vulnerable. I do what I can, but I'm slipping. Even I sometimes drift off by two."

The following morning, when the clock strikes two, she takes up his prayer. "In peace," she repeats, pacing the floor, "will I both lay me down and sleep, for You, O Lord, alone make me dwell in safety."

◊

Tiny bubbles cling to the hair on her arms. She clears a path with her finger, effervescent, prayer reverberating beneath her breastbone in the bath's heat: *in peace, in peace, in peace.*

When she passes her father in the hallway something about him cowers like Helmi after they brought her home, but he stutters, "You look lovely."

Lovely. He has never called her such a thing before.

Bea imagines her prayer—the peace and stillness borne in her through silent repetition—makes it so. The words soften her muscles and joints and unclench her jaw. Her predawn visions have ceased.

On the walk to the spring dance, terns wheel overhead, puddles mirror the dusk, and the air smells of pine. Before going into the celebration hall, she bites a wild cherry and rubs it on her lips.

Passed up and down the line, her bootlaces come undone and then her braids from their crown. She stomps,

115

weaves by Erik's blurred face, Lars and Samuel, twirling Ada, Boe, Samuel again—his dimple flashing like a
wink—Mikael, Erik, the doctor.

"My," says the doctor, pulling her close. "You really
do look just like her."

"Who?" asks Bea. "My mother?" But before he can
answer the dance whisks him away.

Perhaps she wouldn't recognize her father's barely
perceptible recoiling if not for her own, each time Ulrika
enters the room. Her sister is meant to be at home receiv-
ing Oscar—his shaky leg rattling the teacups—when she
appears in Bea's peripheral vision, beside Bruna at the
banquet table, a smudge of blue in the crowd.

But Samuel is watching Bea, too, as he has been for
weeks, and she feels like she could molt and emerge from
the husk of her herself as someone graced and lively and real.

She spins with him out the back door into the orange
sunset, not knowing her dress is soaked with sweat before
the chill air and his arm around her. His breath smells of
hops and honey, and his face is softer than his twin's, and
he is nothing at all like Elias. For a moment they sway out
of time with the music, trampling new plantings, before
she takes his hand and runs with him into the field toward
Lofgren's barn, fireflies blinkering.

They climb a ladder to the hayloft. The sky is gauzy with
stars. Swinging her legs off the edge, Bea pretends she's
not afraid of heights. Below, bedded in their stalls, horses

whinny as fog rolls in, blanketing the celebration hall and the church and homes beyond it. When Samuel kisses her, he grips her chin tight between his thumb and knuckle.

Lying back, straw prickles her neck. Swallows swoop in the rafters. The words murmur away inside her, *Lord, make me dwell in safety.* Samuel's touch is steady and gentle.

When Bea revisits what comes next, she slows the rushed blur of events down beat by beat: Ulrika's face appearing atop the ladder at Bea's feet. Her tentative voice calling, "Beata? Are you alright?"

Bea kicks the top rung.

She will assure herself it was startle reflex, a sharp, involuntary jerking.

The ladder tips, and falls.

Ulrika's body lands with a thump.

Bea screams for help, her sister's shape sprawled in the grass. From the celebration hall, distant fiddles answer. Ulrika stands, weaving, and props the ladder back up.

"Get down from there," Ulrika commands. "Right now." Behind her, lanterns bob in the field's mist, voices shout. Bea's legs shake as she descends.

"It was an accident," she says pitifully, back on solid ground.

"Run," says Ulrika.

Later that night Ulrika creeps down to Bea's bed, nuzzling against her.

"I don't know what got into me," she mumbles, head heavy on Bea's shoulder, eyes closed. Her hair is a thicket of tangles, and the gauze wrapping is damp. "Tell you the truth, I can't stand Samuel. When he tried to kiss me, I bit his tongue." Her words are slurred, as if she talks in her sleep.

"Father can't hear," says Bea. "You don't need to go on pretending."

"What possessed me?" Ulrika asks, childlike, bewildered.

"You hit your head," Bea says. "That was *me*, with Samuel." But Ulrika echoes, "Me."

◊

When Bea ran, staggering through switchgrass, Ulrika stayed to greet her rescuers. From Bea's hiding spot behind Mikael Lofgren's barn, she heard Ulrika exclaim in a bright, trilling voice among the rumble of the men, "What a fool I am. We were exploring the hayloft, and I

slipped." Then the peal of her laughter, long and loose—
the sound of the tavern letting out. The voices faded, and
one of the horses appeared beside Bea at the gate, breath
labored like hers was, mane silver, eyes blinking and wet
with moonlight.

Only afterward would Bea learn that the fall from the
hayloft cracked her sister's head. Samuel carried her back
to the celebration hall, despite her woozy protests, her
blood staining his shirt. There, the music stopped and
the dance floor cleared so the doctor could tend her—he
happened to have his bag. He shaved the back of her head,
and the villagers gathered in a ring around her. The gash
took twenty stitches of bristling black thread.

   "She may be off for a bit," the doctor cautioned when
he delivered Ulrika home, bandaged. "But not to worry.
She'll be herself again soon."

◊

Whispers follow Ulrika like clouds of midges. Bea over-
hears just enough to understand the islanders know what
only Bea and Samuel should. *It's true, Samuel Axelsson
defiled Ulrika in the hayloft. At the spring dance, he put his
fingers inside her.* Bea feels no less exposed, replaced by her
sister. The gossip thickens the air, which presses in on Bea
like water on a diver. Her sister walks with her chin high,
bruises visible and tender.

"None of this would have happened," Bea says, "if you'd left me alone. I can take care of myself."

Ulrika sighs. "Can you?"

◊

"Where is Beata?" asks their father when dinnertime arrives, and Ulrika has not come home.

"Right here," says Bea.

"No, where is *Beata*?" As if he's the one who fell and is concussed.

"You mean Ulrika."

He blinks. "You know who I mean."

Bea tosses pork chops into spattering oil, searing them gray.

"This was how it began," he tells her, before saying grace. "With my mother. Little lapses." His folded hands are white at the knuckles. "One year, forgetting the recipe to her famous rosehip soup. The next, forgetting how to use a spoon. Father built her a pen in the yard, for fresh air." For a long time, he is quiet. "You know, I won't be here forever. I don't know what to do with you girls. Tell me what to do," he begs. Bea searches for an answer, unsure if he is asking her or God.

They wait up for Ulrika, at the table with its uncleared plates of gristle and bone.

At last, the door bangs open and Ulrika sweeps in. Her hair is cropped, short as a man's. Her wound is healing.

Her eyes are bright. "Now who will wed you?" their father asks. She eats scraps from the pan with her fingers.

In the weeks that follow Ulrika is gone more and more, for longer and longer. When Bea asks where, Ulrika says, "Don't worry about me," and Bea thinks of Helmi gone missing and Ulrika saying, "Don't worry, it's an island, how lost could she be," while Helmi was tied up on the Blue Maiden, baying and eating snow. Ulrika has begun wearing their father's old overcoat and cracked leather boots. At twenty, she stands taller than him, the coat draping elegantly from her wide shoulders.

When Bea steals along behind Ulrika, all she does is walk and walk and walk. One night, Bea follows her to the North Cliffs. Another, to Bruna's hut. Bea hides outside in the dark, watching Bruna and Ulrika talk.

As if Ulrika has transformed into her own suitor, she returns before breakfast with a fresh bouquet of lilies and her breath smelling of brännvin, ignoring Bea as she kicks off her boots, propping up her blistered feet like a man making himself comfortable.

"You are on the eve," they sing at Liam Holmberg's funeral, "of lovely summer, when grass and crops grow." Ulrika's voice is overly loud. A snort erupts from her in the silence between verses. Heads turn in the pews. Ulrika rushes up the aisle, face in her hands, shoulders shaking

121

with laughter that will pass for weeping. "Fair land of summer," Bea mouths, "island of wind and sun," but suddenly everything is absurd—the stumbling notes of the organ, the shapes old Wilma Blom, fervent soprano, makes with her mouth. *Don't look*, Bea orders herself. *You are not allowed to look at her.*

At the graveside, ancient Boe Henriksson says to their father, "Ulrika's certainly outgrown you, Silas. Quite the spectacle, isn't she?"

"Pastor Silas, Boe," he answers, smiling. "At least while I'm still in my robe."

Boe chucks their father under his chin. "Oh, you'll always be scrawny Silas to me, trailing after Angelique like her pup." His gaze falls on Bea. "My Lord. This one's her spitting image." He flashes Bea a crooked smile. "Word is, Liam named August his heir. Suppose he'll come back? Suppose we'd better lock up our barns."

"Is that so?" her father answers. "I see." His eyes fill with tears. "I see," he says again. "The Lord never fails to surprise." He tosses a handful of soil onto the casket. "Dust to dust."

"Someone special is coming to dinner," their father tells them. "We must give him our finest welcome."

Their only dinner guest is the bishop, whose yearly supervisory visits sweep through their home like a seasonal gale. While their father describes August Holmberg— nephew to widower Liam one month dead, mainlander and heir to Liam's farm—Bea can't help but picture the bishop, because August seems to make their father equally nervous. "I believe he's done quite well for himself," he says. "And the farm is in fine shape." The Holmberg farm stands alone on the North End's great alvar. Bea knows only how the pastures yellowed after the death of Liam's wife, Nilla, overgrazed by sheep with muddy fleece.

At the butcher's, their father picks out four large pheasants and two bottles of akvavit, though he does not drink.

"My dear," says the butcher's mother, staring at Bea as she ties the pheasants' legs together and packages their bodies. She rounds the counter and takes hold of Bea's hand, her skin sunspotted. "How have you been?" She strokes Bea's knuckles. "You haven't come by for so long." She regards Bea with curiosity and presence, her pupils shaking back

123

and forth. "You look well. You shame the rest of us." The butcher pokes out from the back room, saw in hand, pigs hanging behind him. "Don't let her bother you," he says. "Mother, you're mistaken." Helga's grip tightens. "And your little girl?" she asks fervently. "How is she?" She glances back over her shoulder, as if pursued. "And the baby?" She squeezes Bea's hand painfully. "You must bring the baby by. I won't wait one more day to meet it."

◊

"His ferry must have arrived," their father repeats over and over, each time with fresh concern. He rises to look out the window in the direction of the harbor.

The morning of the dinner, he asks Ulrika to trim his hair. "Like yours, please," he says, as if offering an apology. "Clean me up."

She snips with precision and care, but in the end there are patches where the cut is too close, his scalp visible like Ulrika's at her scar, where the hair has not grown back. He looks at himself in the hallway mirror. "Your spitting image," he says. But Bea knows she's the one who is like him—his tepid plainness watering down her mother's beauty and Viking blood. "I do worry for you," he says, cupping Ulrika's face briefly in his hands.

"And I worry for you," says Ulrika.

At five o'clock, one hour before August is due, Bea comes down to an empty kitchen, warm with the smell of crisped skin, parsnip mash, and turnovers made from the beach's crabapples. The dining table they rarely use is laid with tall, tapered candles and polished silver, at each setting a fluted, thin-stemmed glass. Ulrika, crouching to light the fire, turns and smiles, her front teeth blackened by ash. "Suppose I should meet him like this?"

Bea follows her out to the back field. Ulrika hasn't changed from her apron, splotchy with grease. Blond frizz haloes her face. Bea picks a down feather from her hair. She has never seen her sister cry.

"I suspect he's trying to marry me off," Ulrika says. She smiles, still coal smudged. "Imagine that. You two, making do without me."

In the distance, a rippling cloud of starlings move as one, always knowing when to turn.

Ulrika puts her arms around Bea and pulls her in.

It should make no difference, what the village thinks of Ulrika. She can field dress a rabbit, pluck a pheasant clean, forage mushrooms for stew so savory Bea sneaks cold spoonfuls in the night. Ulrika spends each morning at the spinning wheel, even on Maundy Thursday when folklore says that women who risk it might never be able to halt their spinning. "When do I ever stop?" Ulrika asks Bea warily. If she gives Bea chores, the shell peas roll off the table and the washboard grates her knuckles, so Ulrika does the labor of two—and of mother and father, ripping sloppy stiches from Bea's marriage blanket to mend them,

ANNA NOYES

carrying water from the well eight times a day, shoulders muscled by the yoke. Only in the past weeks has Bea seen her sister take a break of any kind. Even then, at erratic hours, she tends to each task.

She will make a fine wife. The finest.

Back inside, Ulrika lets Bea tuck a sprig of lilac behind her crumpled ear and polish her scuffed boots. Her close-cropped hair brings out her eyes. She unties her apron. Beneath it is a dress the blue of winter mornings.

She is lovely. He will take her.

"Be kind to him," their father says in a rush, when at last the knock comes. He wears a vest with silver buttons and his cheeks have a fresh-shaven sheen. "Be good. My girls."

And then he opens the door, to a tall man who fills the frame.

There you are, Bea thinks. *Finally.*

Ulrika takes August's coat and passes it off to Bea.

Beneath the note of musty wool, his smell lingers on her hands. Earth—like she's been rooting in the garden.

"Look at you," their father says, clapping the heft of August's shoulder. "All grown up. He was practically a boy last I saw him. Twenty years ago?"

He is no boy. He is a man in his forties, Bea guesses, younger than her father.

"Silas," says August, looming over him. "You haven't changed at all."

She has never met anyone who takes up so much space. He nearly turns Ulrika small. Soft curls of hair peak above his shirt collar, whorls of it on his knuckles, his beard threaded with gold. There is something animal about him. She cannot meet his eyes. She recognizes him entirely.

"To our honored guest," toasts her father. A single sip makes her shudder and dulls the taste of things. She has never been allowed to drink. The night is novel. She laughs when the others do, eating the pheasant's skin in one whole strip and the pat of butter off the top of the mash. August cannot seem to look at her, either, though she catches him staring at Ulrika. Bea's stockings are baggy at the knees. Invisible once more, she tries another swallow. When Helmi was alive she slept under the dining table, and Bea would escape the rigid chair to curl alongside her as talk droned overhead. What relief, to slip down unseen like a ring through a hole in a pocket, laying her cheek to the scratchy carpet, surrounded by a barricade of legs.

"Do you really suppose you'll stay?" their father asks. "And try for a life here? Not everyone takes to it."

"I always wanted to come back," says August. He hunches, tracing the tablecloth's vines and crumbs. For such a big man, his voice is almost inaudibly soft. Each time he speaks he winces. "I just hope I won't ruin it."

"Ruin what?" Ulrika says, the lilac behind her ear wilted.

"My fond memories. How well I used to sleep."

Summers on his uncle's farm, the sky stayed light until ten o'clock and he swam every night and had vivid dreams.

"More oxygen in the air," says their father.

"What did you dream?" asks Bea, the first question she has dared.

"Of forking hay"—he smiles—"and shoveling manure." But he woke eager for more of the same. He was nineteen and had never been away from home. Everything thrilled. "So much that happened there doesn't seem real." He clears his throat. "That happened here, I mean." The room encroaches on them—water-stained wallpaper, walls creaking, wind down the chimney—but a vision of the island he wants to come home to has infiltrated Bea's mind, green and shimmering, afterimage of the sun.

"Of course, it has always been real for us," her father says sharply. "We are real."

August nods.

"Even the winters are real," says Ulrika.

"Another toast," says her father. He rises, swaying. "Our *honored* guest." Each syllable is crisp edged. "Up. On your feet."

Before tonight, Bea has never seen him drink more than a sip of communion wine. He has said drunkenness distances a man from God, but she cannot be sure. While parts of her have dimmed, others have come alive. She presses the dip between her collarbones, pulse battering like a moth.

"August." Her father raises his glass, akvavit sloshing the lip. "May you make our home your home. May the island keep you, not spit you out."

"I can hope," murmurs August.

"Terrible luck," her father says. "Toasting without looking at one another."

August's head is bowed.

"Again."

This time, August holds his glass out to Bea.

He looks back at her as if he knows her, too.

His eyes are the lightest shade of green—underside of spring leaves, goatsbeard moss, bloom of algae on the bog.

"I was sorry to hear of your mother's passing," he says.

"You knew her?"

"Not well." Their glasses clink though they're not supposed to, more bad luck, both empty. "I was fond of her. When it rained, sometimes she'd take a lift in the hay cart."

"To the blessed hay cart," says her father, pulling the napkin from his collar and tossing it to the table. "Why don't you and Ulrika go out on the porch and see if you have anything to say to each other."

Alone with Bea, her father draws a sharp breath, like he's readying to jump from the end of the pier. They've pulled chairs close to the parlor's fire, sitting in silence until her dress burns against her legs. "My best girl," he says finally, closing his eyes. "I thought I could bear seeing him again, but he riles me. My spirit is weaker, this past year."

Ulrika's voice, indecipherable, drifts in from the porch.

"I'll tell you, that man was a troublemaker. A pest. One night, during the dance, he got it in his head to steal a horse from Mikael Lofgren's barn. You know Lofgren's horses. Beautifully bred. His pride. He rode her unbridled along the beach but left the gate open behind him and the rest of the horses escaped. No one even knew they were missing until the next morning." His eyes water, as if he is laughing.

"What happened?" she asks, knowing they were swallowed up by the woods or the snow or the ocean. She thinks of a horse walking across the frozen bay, ice breaking, the horse disappearing under. But of course, it was summer. Time for bed.

"I found them," he says, "grazing on buttercups in the grassland. They could have gotten colic. They could have died."

"But did they?"

"No," he says. "Everything was fine. In the end."

They gather on the porch to see August off. He kisses her father's cheek and Ulrika's before leaning down to Bea. "I've solved why you're so striking," he says, mouth grazing her ear. "Your eyes are different colors."

In her bedroom, she tries to focus on the reflection of her face, the image doubled. She closes one eye, then the other. Blue, brown, blue.

They meet for a second time at the market. In daylight August seems younger, white sleeves rolled. A lamb bucks in his arms as he ties on its lead.

"Walk with me?" he asks.

The lamb and August trail her to the grassland. Across the field, spring's growth flushes, new buds on every tree. Wild orange poppies and pasqueflowers grow up through the belly of the stranded skiff. She clambers in, despite the peeling paint and rotting planks. He follows.

"Where are you taking me?" he teases. The grassland ripples like water.

"The Blue Maiden," Bea plays along. "Are you going to marry my sister?"

He reddens to the tips of his ears. "No," he says. "You have the wrong idea entirely." He picks a poppy, twirls it, and offers it to her. "I lied at dinner. I never wanted to live here. I wanted to sell my uncle's farm. Get my affairs in order. Make peace. I liked my life elsewhere. But when your father wrote me"—he shakes his head—"I shouldn't have opened his letter. I shouldn't have come."

She tucks the poppy behind his ear. She cannot help but behave as if he is hers already. "I wanted to meet Ulrika," he says slowly. "But now I've met you, I'm having trouble leaving." He is large in the little boat, his legs crowded against hers. "Small Beata. When I first saw you, I thought I wouldn't survive." It is the first humid day of the season, honeysuckle swarmed with bees, and flies just hatching.

◊

"Marry her?" Her father's voice drifts up from downstairs. "She's practically a girl."

"Nearly Angelique's age," says August, "when you wed her. I'll care for Ulrika, too, once you're gone. As you wished."

"Is this bargain to spite me?"

August sighs. "I'm not the rascal you knew."

"And if I say no?"

"Don't."

For three days, their father shuts himself in his study.

On the fourth, he comes to Bea's door with slippers, dress, and veil crumpled in his arms.

"All these years, I saved these," he says. "For you."

The slippers' soles are gray with her mother's footprints—each toe, the slivers of her arches, the stamps of her heels.

Bea will pad the slippers with kerchiefs to keep them on her feet, but the dress fits her exactly.

"Small Beata," Bea says to herself in the mirror. Her reflection smiles back.

"She's a child," shouts Ulrika when she learns August has asked for Bea's hand. "Look at her," she points, but their father won't. Bea is still wearing her mother's dress. For the first time—she is certain—she looks nothing like a child.

She changes back into her baggy brown shift, reties the two limp braids.

"You don't need to protect me," she says, joining Ulrika on the stoop. Ulrika scans the drive, alert as a guard dog.

"I do," Ulrika says.

"You're just jealous he picked me."

Her sister scoffs.

"I'm not really a child," Bea says. "I'm nearly seventeen."

Ulrika leans on Bea's shoulder. "I was the one who rocked you and bathed you and warmed your milk," she says. "When you were born, your head was bruised. With a soft spot"—she taps the back of her own head—"right here."

◊

Ulrika weaves the crown of Queen Anne's lace.

She tucks their mother's cameo necklace into Bea's packed trunk. "For you," she says. "A wedding gift."

When the procession of village women arrives for Bea, they march her through the grassland to the beach, encircling her at the water's edge, singing and wading in.

134

Bea has watched this ritual from a distance dozens of times, too young to take part. Ulrika recites a passage remembered from the red book: "New bride, taste every dish served at the wedding feast, or else you'll grow insatiable. Walk the aisle in unlaced shoes, so the babe slips from you with ease. On your wedding night, stay awake after the bridegroom, for if you sleep first, you will die first."

"The things people used to believe," sighs Bruna. Her pantlegs are rolled, water lapping her sturdy calves. "So many threats of death, death, death. When won't we die? The fire pops, you die. Dogs dig in your garden, you die. You pick up the wrong stone, dead. An owl hoots at the window, a cow bell rings then ceases, a corpse tilts to the left in its casket, soon you are in a casket, tilting to the left."

Her eyes soften. She squeezes Ulrika's shoulder. "I'm sorry," Bruna says. The sky is dark with an oncoming storm. Old Sophie wrings out the cloth. "Let me," says Ulrika.

"You're unmarried," protests Widow Ingrid as the others resume their singing.

Ulrika kneels in the sand. She washes Bea's feet.

◊

Bea's slippered feet don't look like her own. They shuffle along, veil sliding behind. Villagers, flanking the aisle, are less real through the web of lace. The walls ripple with weak late-afternoon light. The church watches, breathes,

135

reverberates with the sounds that have rung out there over one thousand years. Rain taps the roof. Bea shakes. At the altar, August takes hold of her hands, though it is custom not to touch.

"This union," says her father, "is a bulwark against depravity. Marry not for lust but for love and children. A wife is a helper, made for man by God. In marriage, the home is a fortress and the homelife sacred. To cook and clean in service of a family is a holy, ordained task. Be faithful to that labor, to one another. What is marriage, if not a vessel for our faith, an unwavering commitment to chastity and decency. If we break our vow, we break not only from our husband or wife but from God and our very life." He pauses, then resumes, addled, with the sermon of a boat disappearing on one horizon and appearing on another.

When music fills the celebration hall, August pulls her in without shaking off the rain. So close to his face, she forgets her steps. She has never seen a man more beautiful—*handsome* is not quite right, despite his beard and breadth, crooked nose and eyebrow bisected by a scar—but she can't be sure others are struck by him, too. It doesn't matter. He moves with grace, skirting her clumsiness, and she relaxes against him, swinging back and forth, spinning until queasy. His neck tastes of salt. Her feet skim the ground.

*

"Where are you taking me?" asks August, laughing as he stumbles through the field.

Water climbs her hem. The slippers are soaked and flecked with grass. At Lofgren's barn, she says, "Steal a horse for me?"

"Who told you that?" He looks slapped. "Silas?"

Had he agreed, she would have left the wedding right then to ride with him through the surf.

"I'm only teasing."

"Don't," he says. "That night embarrasses me."

In the hayloft she undoes his buttons, rolls down her stockings. "Wait." He closes his eyes, presses his forehead to hers. "I thought we might wait."

He is gentle until she is ungentle.

Her father stands in the entry of the celebration hall. Over the course of the day all boyishness has drained from his face, as if twenty years have caught him at once: softened chin, slack cheeks, long earlobes. Bea straightens his glasses. He eyes her like a cornered rabbit.

"When I first saw your mother sitting in my church pew, I thought she was God's gift," he mutters. "The companion I'd prayed for. Better to marry than to burn, the Bible says. Forty years old, and I'd never found a wife to love on this island. All that time burning, alone, God granted me no peace. Luther warned this state could only lead to the most heinous sins. But I hadn't committed them. And then your mother arrived, so alert, so *vivid*,

137

and *Be fruitful and multiply* rang out inside me, and for once in my life I knew just what God wanted.

"But it was marriage, after all, that led to my most heinous sins," he says. "She was a child with a sick mother looking toward a life alone, in need of a priest's counsel. And all I saw was a vessel for my own joy, and I claimed it. I should never have married her."

"Thank you for today, Father," says August, coming up behind Bea. "For our union." He kisses her temple and picks a hay straw from her hair.

"Be happy," says her father, like a warning. He begins to cry. "Take care of each other. She is my daughter."

Part IV

S he does not know the room she wakes to: low ceil-inged, sunless, ironing board draped with a starched white shirt. *If only I could retrace my steps*, she thinks, *I'll know why I'm here.* But behind the one blankness lurk numerous others.

What she knows is the room is off somehow, like fresh milk gone sour, filling her with disquiet that teeters on the edge of panic.

She walks out into snow. It does not matter where the road takes her.

Minutes pass or, perhaps, hours. Her nightgown drags through slush. A carriage slows. "Are you alright, Madam?" asks the driver, leaning out the window on a hairy forearm. Who he is—and all of it—seems on the tip of her tongue, as if she's merely lost the thread for one beat, midconversation. How to explain? She doesn't know her own name.

"Do you need a lift somewhere? Back home?"

"I'm quite alright," she says crisply, and it seems she will be, so long as she keeps moving, though she can't say where home is either. "I'm just clearing my head." Her gait quickens, her mind clear as can be, an empty room swept by spring breeze.

If not for the island's inevitable border, she could have kept walking until her hair tangled and her nails grew long, untroubled by the cold, the slippers turning to tatters on her feet, as driven to go as the willow warbler following its migratory urge.

But the row of houses and the laughter of villagers, eyeing her at a distance, return her to herself. Enough so, in any case, to feel ashamed.

The walk back to the Holmberg farm, from one end of the island to the other—nearly five miles—ends with the sun glaring and high overhead. Crossing the alvar, Bea's slippers are soggy, so it is difficult to run. And there on the stoop waits August, alarmed at the sight of her stumbling in her thin, nearly translucent nightgown, insistent the doctor come even as she insists through chattering teeth that it is nothing, really, all is well. "I just needed to clear my head," she explains, panting, though she wonders if in fact she has been sleepwalking while portions of her mind remain awake and alert. It is easier to tell August, "A headache. Cold air, I thought, would make it better."

This isn't how things are meant to unfold, the doctor Bea's first guest as lady of the house.

In the chilly parlor, Bea accepts a single, medicinal swallow of sherry but turns down the doctor's morphine pills and tucks into the armchair. Its wings block her view of August and the doctor, who speak across her of a new bride's easy exhaustion.

"Are these headaches frequent?" the doctor asks. "Perhaps she's been unduly stressed?" Before she can answer, he continues, "You must take care of your young wife."

August pats her knee.

The words *new bride* and *young wife* still carry the delicious charge of costuming for a masked ball, seven weeks in.

The doctor leans forward to scrutinize her face. "Beata," he says. "You put me in mind of Angelique, traipsing the island when she was meant to be nursing her mother. Poor girl, she learned her lesson. Don't run yourself ragged like your mother did."

When she and August are alone again, as they have been for the past seven weeks, they stretch out on his bed. He lays his head in her lap.

"I worried you'd left me already," he tells her.

Each time he looks up, even when his face is tucked between her legs, his eyes go faintly crossed. This is one of the myriad things about him that strikes her as singularly wonderful. She loves, without reservation, the lanolin-like sheen his skin leaves on her lips, the stink of his work boots, his many silvery cowlicks.

Her fingers rub his scalp in slow circles, his head growing heavier and heavier in her lap. How clear that her touch comforts. His eyes close. She smooths his furrowed forehead with her thumb, his mouth pursing in sleep. Light beams toward him from the center of her chest. Despite her failings and frequent selfishness, moments like this with August let her glimpse the good mother she could one day become: protective, fierce, unified, and whole. Transformed.

His eyes open, their pale green startling like so much about him. A rush of happiness passes over her, like the bright crest of a wave.

"You're a snake charmer," he murmurs.

"You're a snake." She kisses the curve of his ear.

Each time she pulls her hand away he wakes, and so she keeps running her fingers through his hair, until pinky to thumb they fall asleep.

Everything is fresh and bright and pleasing once more, the fire popping, a log settling, the steps that carried her here easily retraceable. *I am home*, she thinks, and when the subtlest stirring of unease returns, this time it is not rooted in the room but inside her, low in her belly, its features just forming as if it were the beginnings of a baby, no larger than a pearl.

The sheep make her laugh, such plump, wooly bodies and small legs. Even the words *sheep farm* comfort, sounding like a place to settle. She collects the still-warm eggs, pale green and blue, from beneath the hens. The horses eat crabapples from her palm. The Holmberg farmhouse sprawls, its thatched roof muting the sound of rain. She takes luxurious midday naps in the room that was meant to be hers alone, in a broad bed with a yellow coverlet. When August first showed her to the guest room, he looked at her startled. "Oh no," he said. "She's sad already."

She kissed his chest. "I thought we'd share a bed."

He had carried her down the hallway to his bedroom as she laughed and squealed, and thrown her on his unmade bed. Straw poked through the mattress. She took him between her legs, wanting to shelter him from her disappointment, like a boat gently rocking in the safety of a harbor.

"All I want," he said against her neck, "is a little son by you. All I want is you, and our son."

He teases that she turns the sheets to a swamp with her sweating and kicks him in the night.

"But you may stay," he says. "Please stay," kissing her palms, the soles of her feet. Lifting her nightgown, he kisses her stomach and whispers a prayer against it.

In the daytime, she walks place to place in a daze. Miles up island from the village center, the adjacent great alvar is like a desert. She gathers seaweed on the shore for his fields. He props her against the splintering slats of the barn. He pulls her into his cool and silty bathwater. She runs her fingers down the seam of hair that trails from his bellybutton, like those she rips. She is loose limbed, blunted, careless, worked like the dough she kneads as his seed runs down her thigh. His beard scabs her chin, and each day the scab is freshly reopened. Her lips are swollen, hair tangled. Thank God for the farm's isolation, the house empty of servants. The sounds she makes.

When he leaves for the fields in the morning, and when he returns grimy at night, they hold each other. She tucks easily into him. Still damp from the day's work, he smells of peat and sap and ocean. Like the island itself.

She lays the table for two, lights the sputtering wicks, seasons supper with his long-dead aunt's ancient collection of brittle indistinguishable herbs. She adds flour until the dough turns pliable. Home from the field, he puts his arms around her. She has just turned seventeen. She is a woman. The word quickens and calms her both. Women are rooted. He lifts her skirts. She braces herself against the counter as he guides himself inside her. He breathes against her hair.

"Angelique," he says.

Her hands slip in the flour.

For an instant, she sees the kitchen around her and the house beyond it, a widower's home: skittering in the walls, black mold on the bed ruffle, hearths spilling ash, parlor ferns draped in dust, rusted frying pans, reeking mouse nests, weevils in the oats, raccoons in the cellar, fingernail parings, sinks clogged with hair, shut-up rooms stacked with fabric cut for dresses never sewn, hundreds of mildewed patchwork quilts, moldering heaps of raw wool.

He kisses the nape of her neck. "Beata, my Beata, my Beata."

Returned for a monthly dinner, Bea tries to tell her father and Ulrika of her new life, its sweetness.

"Go on, taunt me more with how happy you are," her father says, his voice jagged. For the first time since she arrived, she takes him in closely. His face is carved down to a gaunt shape. "You'd make a fool of me. From the moment I saw you, you made me your fool."

"Be careful," says Ulrika. "You are not yourself."

"Me?" asks Bea.

"Him," mouths Ulrika, with their father looking on. "I'm glad you're enjoying it. Playing house."

"Parading around in your green dress," he says, a startling hatred in his voice. "It's too much." He puts his face in his hands. "It is cruel. You have always been cruel. My God. My God," he says again, rising. "I've got to untie the dog. I've forgotten the dog."

"What dog?" asks Bea.

And he says back, "The dog, I've got to . . ." But then he trails off. "I apologize. I've slept poorly. Thank you for supper. It was delicious."

The meal Ulrika cooked sits before them, untouched and steaming.

148

He looks down at his heaped plate, up at Bea in terror. He covers her hand with his own. "Beata," he says. "You've been missed."

Before Ulrika takes her back to August's, Bea kisses her father's cheek. The buttons of his coat are misaligned, one side hanging longer than the other. He lets her do them up correctly, like a mother preparing her child for snow.

I do love it here, Bea thinks to say as they approach the farmhouse, its windows dark.

Stepping down from the carriage she asks, "What is happening to him?" Ulrika does not know. Perhaps he is losing himself, as his mother did. He has insisted to Ulrika, lately, that at last God is exacting sin's penalty.

The question echoes and warps in Bea's mind: *What is happening to me? What is happening to me?*

"I'm dreaming," says August, still half-asleep. "There were two of you."

"What did we do, us two?"

"Charged me. Bared your teeth."

"We wouldn't." She bites down lightly on his shoulder. "Was I afraid?"

"I was."

"Do you think of her often?" she asks, rubbing his back.

"Who?" murmurs August. "Ulrika?"

"Why would you think of Ulrika?" She pulls her hand away. "*Do* you think of Ulrika?"

"No."

"But you think about my mother."

"You look like her," he answers. "Less so, the more I know you. That's all that was."

She wants to know exactly how. Hair splayed across the pillow, she waits for him to say something of their beauty.

It's in the way Bea gesticulates when she speaks, he says, propping up on his elbow, but also smaller things. The ridges on her fingernails. Like Bea, Angelique had hips that canted forward, slouched shoulders, and small, pointed ears. He examines Bea unreservedly but also looks beyond her as if she is translucent, a sketch on tracing paper overlaying the original, full-color picture. "Your nostrils flare when you are angry," he says. "Your voices are the same but not your laughter."

"I thought you barely knew her."

"I didn't."

"It seems you did."

"From a distance." He waves the thought away. "It hardly matters. I was nineteen. We were children."

"But I am seventeen," says Bea. "And I love you."

She wants to know particulars.

He tells her of Angelique's tangled hair, a missing eyetooth, a freckled face. From the farm, he watched her exploring the alvar with Bruna. He offered her lifts back to the inn. Around her, he struggled to speak. She loved to tease. He was gullible. He believed everything she said. Once after church she confessed she liked his singing voice. Her teasing was akin to lying.

"I couldn't carry a tune," he says. "I should have known better. She probably told everyone nice things like that. She was open. In any case, I was nothing to her. By summer's end, she belonged to your father."

◊

The sheep have twigs and leaves and dirt clots in their wool. They scatter when she follows them through pasture to the cove, incoming tide like another fence. When she collects the hen's warm eggs, the black-eyed cockerel flies up to roost in her hair, claws tickling. In the kitchen garden, she unearths a bounty of parsnips, white roots gnarled like Bruna's arthritic fingers. They are light and dry as good kindling, after winter underground. She slices them to coins, pops one in her mouth, spits it back out. She sleeps with a sachet of cedar under her pillow to ward off moths.

Through the bedroom window, she watches August unpin sheets from the line. They fall to the grass. They are still wet when she gathers them, covered in bits of dried leaves. "They were dirty," he says over dinner. His job is a tidy woodpile, hers a clean laundry line. She washes them again. It's true, there are many faint stains—stubborn and set—her own blood. It always comes as a surprise, though it arrives steadily, month by month, with each new moon.

Their chances of conception are improved, he thinks, if they couple only in bed with Bea on her back.

"Don't move so much," he says, as she links her ankles behind his hips. He puts a hand over her mouth. She licks his palm.

One night she wakes herself shouting, "Do you see it? Do you see it?"

"See what?" he asks, panicked. "Where?" He is on his feet, ready to greet an intruder.

A mosquito hawk as big as the bed hovers over them, its sucker teasing at her throat like a sword.

Five weeks pass, six, moon waxing and waning and she does not bleed. It isn't food that nauseates, but inanimate objects. The cattle horn comb raking back her hair.

She takes a wet rag to each hardened spill, scraping with her thumbnail. Even the candlesticks are grease coated. She wipes the mouths of jars. A single dropped dried currant lures battalions of ants.

The witch comes for children who hide sweepings beneath their bed. Laziness and greed and grief lure her, and like ants streaming in after one linty currant she senses each slip and lapse through the walls, at a distance. Locked out, she rattles the glass.

*

"What are you singing?" asks August.

It's been the same song for days, maybe months. The maypole song. She sings louder. Little frogs without ears, without tails.

When he smiles, she does the dance, wriggling her fingers at her temples, flapping her hands at the base of her spine, hopping toward him. "Stop that," he says, but she keeps dancing until he laughs and she is out of breath. At once, she knows the song is for the creature inside her, though she pictures it more like a tadpole, eyeless and limbless, with a flicking tail. "You're being a child," he says, pulling her into his lap. "Bless our baby," he whispers in her ear. "Bless our house."

In the morning there is blood. She cleans her thighs.

August stays in bed, as if he's the one unwell. "It was your dancing," he says.

"It was not."

He lets her hold him.

"I'm sorry," he says at last, just as she's about to. "Forgive me."

Late winter brings beetles. Their cloverlike smell blooms when she crushes them. She keeps a tiny orbit around the cookstove's warmth, hours spent generating then tidying her own mess. August, cheeks pink from cold, asks after her day. What to tell him? She teeters along a tightrope strung between his leaving and his return.

When he is gone, she wears his dirtied work shirt. It comes down to her knees. She buries her face in the armpit like it is an ether rag.

She thinks all the time of his hands—rasp of calluses on her skin, nails packed with dirt—and all they can do, picking hooves and tying thief knots, splitting wood and building caskets, hooping barrels and digging wells.

And when he is near, she wants to tunnel right into him, like a bark beetle burrowing into spruce. It's the same urge even when he is inside her, like she can never get close enough, like they are never quite touching. These days, he keeps his eyes closed.

"I miss you," she tells him, tracing shapes between the freckles on his back, new constellations.

"I'm right here."

"Don't you ever feel that way? Missing someone you're with?"

"No," he says. "The people I miss are dead."

He has stopped kissing her mouth. Instead, each morning and night he gives her cheek a single peck.

"Easy," he says when she kisses him, gentling as if she is a bucking, untrained animal.

During their sex, while she lies motionless, he wraps his fingers loosely around her throat. She guides the hand down, but it drifts up again.

◊

Thirteen months after their wedding, she draws the privacy curtain and shimmies back into her marriage gown. It hangs differently—slack in some parts, tight in others. The studio is cold, her feet bare. Her palms sweat as if she's at the doctor's office, and there's a faint ammoniac smell. "Come on out, love," the photographer says. "No time to waste here." He hands her a bouquet of frayed silk lilies. The daguerreotype is a wedding gift; it's taken them this long to escape the island. But August has refused to change into his groom's suit.

"No one wants to look at an old man," he says like he is doing her a favor, settling behind the camera. "I'd rather look at you."

"Hold still," says the photographer as Bea straightens her shoulders. Her head is held still by a clamp. Twice more her blood has stopped, then started again. Her sleep troubled, she has resumed her neglected nightly prayer—silently reciting the words now, hoping to feel centered. She makes the face she practiced, one to watch over her son from the mantle.

"You won't want to be smiling," the photographer says. "If you move, you'll ruin the image. You know, when children won't stop wriggling, I tie them down."

There is a hook in her throat.

She tries to conjure love for the son she might bear but has no inkling of him. If only she could imagine a crying baby, the relief of orienting to someone who needs her entirely. But August is encompassing. Still. And painfully dear: as he cleans his plate of her oily gravy with his thumb at the speed of someone starving, or when she opens the cookstove to find his toasting boots, or when, exhausted, he buries his head in her lap.

The photographer sighs. "That will have to do."

The woman that develops wears a mask of Bea's face, mouth downturned, features crooked but crisp. She is devoid of complex inner aliveness. The photographer colors in her cheeks. What surrounds her seems thicker than air, mottled and flecked, like the hornet trapped in amber the teacher one time let Bea hold.

They are in the same city where Elias went to boarding school eight years before. Sheltered from the wind by

August, she spots Elias in the street. Her instinct is to hide, to turn and run as if trespassing. But it is not him after all, only a woman with short hair and delicate stature. She goes on mistaking others for him—a hobbling, ancient man, a boy no older than ten, the age he was when he left.

She does not know if they would recognize each other now.

At the hotel she drinks too much wine, kissing and tugging at August, undressing to her slip. "I need air," he says, but he pins her to the floor, puts his head between her thighs, licks her. How good this used to feel. Now it shames her. When she reaches down to stroke his hair, he pushes her hand away and holds it firm.

"Is this what you want?" he says, tongue flicking sharp against her though she thinks he is trying to please her, a twinge of pain like a tooth's root exposed to cold. "Is this what you want from me?"

◊

Bea recalls August's aunt and uncle as austere and gray—the aunt especially, hands clasped as if always praying, braid thick but her part wide, a sheen to her scalp. Before moving in with August, Bea expected the home they once inhabited to be similarly stark. Instead, room upon room is filled to the brim with years of accumulated mess. Now, one by one, she's decided it's time to reclaim them. She weaves a path through mattresses spilling stuffing, dress

157

molds, felt feathered hats she could punch back into shape, a stringless loot, a loom, a crib though August was their only heir. In the corner, a portrait of a young woman stares from inside a gilded frame.

The figure in the painting wears a necklace, its pendant a woman's profile carved in white against blue. Bea's mother's necklace.

For one dizzying moment, at last, Bea and her mother are face-to-face.

She searches for herself in the pointed chin and small mouth, the high forehead and auburn hair. The painting gazes lovingly back, dabs of light in each green iris.

And then Bea flips the canvas to find the aunt's name scrawled in charcoal. It is not her mother after all, only the dour aunt, when she was still peachy and luminous.

Bea feels each swallow against the choker's ribbon. Her mother's silver ring is tight on her finger, worn in place of her wedding band. She slides into bed beside August, lacing their fingers together.

"Where did you get that?" August sits up, taking her in. "And the necklace?"

"You liked me in her wedding dress," Bea says sharply.

His eyes are wide with distress. "I gave her that necklace. The ring."

"Tell me what happened."

"An engagement ring," he answers. "I wanted to marry her."

"She turned you down?"

"Rightly so. I was a boy, wayward like your father said. I stole the jewelry from my aunt. She looked for that necklace for weeks. But she didn't miss the ring. It's just a cheap piece of nickel."

Bea twists the band. The initials etched inside, mysterious her whole life long, must be his aunt and uncle's.

"She refused me. You did not. Are you happy?"

Bea is quiet. For once, she does not want to know more.

"Take it off," he says. "Now. Please."

"No."

He stares, startled.

"I'm afraid I've made a grave mistake. You're nothing like her, are you?"

◊

For a full year, she had dozed in the crook of his arm. Her waking dreams woke him. Each morning, the sheets were damp, as if just yanked off the line.

It turns out, after all, he prefers the luxury of sleeping alone.

She moves into the guest room, with a wide bed all her own. But each night, she returns to August. The hallways are dim and windowless and rangy. The carpets are threadbare where feet have scuffed but otherwise plush. Lying under August—inert and comfortably crushed—is

159

one more thing to crave. She wakes herself knocking on a door. The house is large enough to get lost in. In the morning her knuckles are tender. She wakes to him inside her and cannot rise out of that submerged place, dark and lowdown as the bottom of a well. Beetles scurry out from under her when she rolls over. Beside the bed, a woman rides a spotted horse. Her face is blurred. She smiles broadly. She has no teeth.

Bea chooses one of the aunt's hats, green with pheasant feathers in its band.

The world is brightly lit, like the one she emerged into after her poisoning, muscles softer and new tips on the pines. Far off, August's small shape tends his flock. The doctor has advised she walk no farther than the property's length.

She passes the prescribed boundary without glancing back, the driveway's mouth grinning behind her.

At the water, wind steals her hat. It floats along, keeping pace, taken by the tide before she can wade in.

The grassland's juniper brush is freshly burnt, pockets of smoke still rising through the damp. Fog lines the ditches. Ghosts come in fog, the villagers have always said.

"Hello," she calls to the tall, thin house. Empty. Its bones creak and pop.

Ulrika's bed is unchanged from childhood, the same sandy sheets and sunken mattress. Her sister's name is carved on the headboard in jagged letters, each repetition smaller and fainter than the last, like an echo. Any minute, the girls they used to be could arrive with their warm milks, her presence nothing to them but a chill.

Bea is aware of the sheet's gentle drape, the veined glow of her closed eyes even as she travels elsewhere, to the kitchen. There, she watches a woman's back. Seated at the table, the woman sings, "Now the Time of Blossoming Arrives." She wears a thick red braid. She does not hear footsteps coming up behind her. She does not take Bea in. Heavily pregnant, she shells peas and eats the pods. Her eyes are clear, with crow's feet at their corners. Bea tucks the reedy timbre of her mother's voice away inside her, her freckled hands, the sunburned rims of her ears, how she pats her foot out of time with the song. Her voice is hoarse, as if she's been singing, seated, nimble fingered, for years. Bea is afraid to leave her.

But she does. She is still in Ulrika's bed, her father—home, after all—pacing below.

"The heart is deceitful above all things," he says, sermon voice rising, on the bottom bunk to her top bunk. "Deceitful, above all. And desperate. And desperately wicked."

He takes the stairs.

Last Sunday, instead of speaking he left the pulpit for a pew, where he knelt and prayed. The congregation joined him—for some hours together they were quiet—but the bishop has been summoned, and his replacement will surely be suggested soon.

"Beata," he says, unsurprised, as if he has been waiting.

He sits beside the bed in the rocker with sagging wicker. Fingerprints smudge his glasses.

"Back to your own bed," he says, smoothing her hair. She is unsure which version of her he sees, if he speaks to her child self.

"Just one minute more," says Bea. "Tell me a story."

The chair runners creak. "When Helmi was a puppy," he says, "she slept between your mother and me. I let her chew my ears. Your mother sang her songs. When Ulrika was a baby, she'd yank Helmi's whiskers. Or maybe the whisker puller was you. Her lip stretched, like this." He tugs his own white-stubbled cheek, the inside of his mouth glinting pink and dark. "But she never once growled." Bea's scalp prickles. "Helmi reminded me too much of your mother. I took her to Blockula."

"Not this story," Bea says.

"I left her to die."

"You're confused," she says, though the look he gives her is not confusion or fear but a lucid kind of hope.

"Maybe you know this already? And the rest of it? Your mother? Did I already tell you?" He rocks. "A song, then. One minute more."

◊

When Ulrika told the tale of the island's witches, Bea knew the sound of fingers tapping glass, the feel of contorting oneself to sneak into a house by any means, the crunch of bone and strain of ligament so the witch woman might fit the chimney pipe or slip under the door. She has always thought the story passed down by her mother, an outsider's pull toward local legend—the stolen babes, the journey to the Devil's island. The men deliberating day and night before taking up their tools. The women marched to their death in the grassland. She knows well the blank faces of the boys and men surrounding them.

It occurs to her perhaps the story was her father's after all, told to Ulrika before Bea's time.

◊

Dozens of hands sweep Bea's cheeks, hair, mouth. They stroke her as Bea used to pat Helmi, the dog unable to slink away, ears flattened, touch like a windstorm. She cannot get her eyes to open.

"Wake up."

For a moment, she is unmoored by Ulrika, sitting on the bed beside her. But she is back in August's house, after all, where she is meant to be, where she went to bed. The sky outside the window is already blue. Her sister is real. The change in the day's monotonous course feels like Christmas morning.

"Beata," Ulrika says. "Father is dead."

*

They found his rowboat before they found his body, drifting untethered and oarless in the harbor. His compass wet
in the bow. Ulrika swaddled it with her shawl.

"He was headed for the Blue Maiden," Ulrika says.
"He thought Helmi was still there." In the days before,
increasingly disoriented, he'd laid in bed muttering, "I left
her to die. I left her to die." Ulrika sat vigil beside him.
"God should not forgive me," he told her. She placed a
straw cross over his heart and he held it. "Who are you?"
he whispered. "You are not my daughter."

"Why didn't you send for me?" Bea asks.

"To spare you seeing him like that."

Laid out in the parlor, he wears the sleeping gown
he washed ashore in.

Bea covers his legs with a blanket. Ulrika combs
sand from his hair. The doctor hovers but does not help
with the impossible task of dressing him and putting on
his shoes.

All afternoon heaped plates are placed in Bea's lap,
then removed. Logs settle to ash. Waves crash. Her father
does not stir. The house crowds with guests, empties.
"Where's August?" Bea asks.

"Gone home," Ulrika says. "He didn't want to wake
you."

Bea has no memory of falling asleep.

In the bedroom, Ulrika tells her, "Arms up," and Bea
obeys, dress off, nightgown slipped over her shoulders.

165

Under the covers, she faces the wall. There is pressure and heat in her chest, peat compacting to coal.

"I remember the days after our mother died," Ulrika says.

He is not there to tell her she can't possibly remember, so Bea says it for him. The words come out like a snarl.

"He wouldn't leave her bed," Ulrika says. "Stopped eating. Grew delirious, like he was this past year. Left me to care for you. He said he was going to hell, that he was there already. He told me he was burning."

Bea wailed in her crib from the moment she was born, Helmi howling with her. Finally, Ulrika warmed milk as the village women had shown, testing its temperature on her wrist, skimming off the skin. When Bea took to the bottle at last, ravenous, the new quiet seemed to draw him out.

He locked her bedroom door. He hid the key.

"I ran from him," Ulrika says. "I don't know why. The road cut my feet. I went to Bruna's. Why? She fed me and wrapped me in a blanket. She said the moment our mother died, she felt her sweetness and sadness return to the world. 'Now she's everywhere,' she promised. I wanted none of it. I only wanted her." Ulrika reaches for Bea. "I had you."

It's true, Bea has sensed her mother—her mother if not God—in the island's sweet offerings: snowdrops blooming during February thaw, microcosmic forests of reindeer lichen, turtles lined on a log in the pond from large to small, sunning their shells. And she's sensed her, too, in slick-walled caves, crows taking flight with viscera in their beaks, cattle bones in the tilled fields, hundreds of opalescent jellyfish washing ashore, lovely as moonstone before they begin to reek.

Bea cannot help but listen for her father's footsteps.

It was his house, never theirs.

Soon a mainland priest will arrive to bless the body. He will take over the church and with it the house. It is a priest's house.

"Where will you go?" Bea asks.

"Nowhere," says Ulrika. "I'll haunt this place until I die."

"Me too," says Bea. "And then?"

"I could go anywhere."

Ulrika's arm is tight around her. Bea feels a spark of joy—girlish, untimely, and ungainly—that she had thought snuffed out. Tonight, the house belongs to them.

Ulrika cuts across August's field. Wrapped in a blue shawl, she is bright in the wheat's gold. He leans on his rake, waiting. When they meet, they hold one another. Then Ulrika unwinds the scarf and runs her fingers through her chopped hair. For too long they talk and pace, and when Bea approaches, they hush.

It is clear Ulrika has been crying.

She has brought along a pail of cold pork loin, applesauce, and tea cake.

"But I thought I would cook," Bea says.

"Save that for lunch, then," says Ulrika and sets about salting the roast. "Didn't I ever teach you to chop onions?"

"What is it I'm doing?"

Bea's eyes sting, knife in hand. A fleck of papery onion skin has wedged under her thumbnail, purple and tender. Ulrika selects another from the bin, undoing it in seconds. She adds a thick pat of butter to the pan Bea is warming. The onions sizzle and sweat.

"Let me," Bea says.

"What good is happening in here?" August asks, coming in at dusk.

"Bea whipped up a feast," Ulrika says, spooning her applesauce onto their plates.

"Best meal you've ever made." He grazes the small of Bea's back and she opens, petals to sun. Then he takes his hand away to squeeze Ulrika's arm.

"I knew I was right," he says. "You're stronger than any field hand."

"August," says Ulrika. "I can't."

"I told her I could use her help here. There's more than enough room. She'd be doing me a favor." His touch returns to Bea. "It's what Silas would have wanted. I imagine you could use a helper, too. A bit of company."

Bea smiles, teeth sharp in her mouth.

She has pictured Ulrika shuttling up and down the stairs of the tall, thin house, cooking Sunday dinners for the next priest and the next, serving plums to the bishop, growing old and bent in her girl's bed.

"That's kind," Ulrika says to Bea, as if it is her kindness. "But I'll take care of myself. I always have. I won't trouble you."

"No trouble at all," he says. "We were getting lonely."

The bouquet of pussy willow branches Bea gathered for the table's center seems embarrassing now, like kindling. She tosses it on the fire.

In the sink full of oily dishwater, Ulrika's hand brushes against Bea's, slippery as an eel. "I *could* help you," she says. "Carry a child, I mean. Care for you. If that's what you want."

"He told you?"

"He worries for you."

On the parlor piano, August plunks the same progression of chords.

"We both do," Ulrika says. "Bruna's taught me some. I could make a tincture. I'll leave after the birth."

"I've got the bridge," calls August. "Perfect for Ulrika's range. Won't you sing?"

His face shines as they settle by the fire.

"Only if Bea joins me," says Ulrika.

As girls, they sang so loudly together the strings on the lute buzzed. Alongside Ulrika, Bea can cleave to the pitch, dissonance slipping toward harmony, two voices merging into one that is rich and brassy and clear. They used to drive their father mad.

"She can do many things," August says, patting the crown of Bea's head. "But sing, she cannot."

So this is what he looks like when he is happy. It has been months.

When he begins to play, Ulrika closes her eyes. She sings of a man traveling a heathery moor to get back to his love.

An unwelcome thought arises.

Only when Ulrika dies will Bea live individuated and capable, for maybe a few years before her own death.

She has ensconced herself in August's home, in August, in wifedom, the farm a barricade. But sitting so close to her sister in August's parlor—the thought of living together again broached—Bea feels the tug of riptide. She is once more the little sister. Ulrika's beast. Ulrika's ward. The sanctuary of the new life and family Bea was trying to build this past year has been breached. Ulrika is her family, the primacy of that earliest bond forever fated to win out.

Under her breath, she sings out of time, out of tune, louder, and August eyes her.

For a moment she can sense a future self. Her father and Ulrika and even August gone, and a weight holding steady in her center, like a keel.

◊

Bea sews crooked curtains for the tenant cabin's windows. There is a cookstove for warmth, dead flies in a copper kettle, horsehair and moss insulation and glimpses of light between the logs. Ulrika insists, if she is to stay, on living here instead of the main house.

When Bea lies back on the cot it is like lying in a field, laced with the scent of wildflowers and cedar, the vestigial funk of the boys who once slept there, a mourning dove cooing so loudly it might have built its nest in the bedframe. As if the future has arrived, the tiny space belongs briefly to Bea, not to Ulrika. The field is hers and

171

the farm, the island, and her body, and she wonders why she hasn't come here all along. "I insist," she says to the cabin's quiet. "I insist."

◊

On the hillside, August and Ulrika's twin forms are broad shouldered and tall, with light in their hair.

Ask and Embla. Adam and Eve.

She flips through August's diary for her name, but all she finds is: *planted field; cut hay; 2 lambs, 3 chicks; shelled peas, last corn; threshed barley.*

In the evenings, Ulrika moves briskly about the kitchen redoing what Bea has done, a sharp smell wafting behind her like August's before sponging clean. As when they were girls, instead of helping, Bea dips her cup straight into the churn for buttermilk flecked with fat. Ulrika's molds transform cold butter into oak leaves and acorns.

August delights at the melting leaf on his mash, as if the stamp were created just for him.

"Laid another blue one for you," he says shyly at dawn, tucking a speckled green-blue egg into Ulrika's napkin.

Across the breakfast table, Bea takes in her sister's strong jaw, sharp chin, wide mouth and deems her brutish, just like her schoolmates said. Three faint lines, early wrinkles, cut across her throat.

*

172

Ulrika's tincture is the silty green-brown of the shallows where they used to wade barefoot, digging oysters.

"What's in it?" Bea asks.

"Oat flower. Cramp bark."

"What does it do?"

"Calms the womb," Ulrika says. "Your nerves."

She makes August a salve for his dry elbows, his smell supplanted by fir balsam, molasses, mutton tallow, lily root, and rosin.

"I thought you finished with all that," Bea says. "After you poisoned me."

"Not quite," Ulrika smiles. "It turns out the red book lives in my head, too. I know the species our mother added better than I know the islanders, what's gone, what's gained. We've lost chokecherry, rose pogonias. I won't bore you." August listens, enthralled. "Now we have beach plums. Wild lovage once grew on every shore. I've looked for it for years. Then yesterday I found it, right where it should be, in a shady spot at the mouth of a spring."

"You remind me of her," August says. "Angelique."

Alone in bed, Bea listens to their distant laughter.

When the cabin door slams, she goes to August.

"I don't make you laugh," she says.

"No one does." There is a long, charged silence that gives her goose bumps. "Look," he says. "If you want, I'll laugh at you. I only laugh when people expect it."

173

"How can you tell they expect it?"

"The light in their eyes."

◊

August flips a ewe onto her back. She stills instead of struggling, eyes wet and wide. The blade sheers snip. He says softly, "Easy, easy, easy." Bea watches from the barn door, a clover mite, red and tiny as a pinprick, tickling up her arm.

"Now you try," he says to Ulrika.

She comforts in the same way—"Easy, easy"— shearing fleece as effortlessly as she skins apples in one long strip. "You're a natural," August says.

Bea's back aches, her breasts. As always, she is sickened lately by innocent things, Ulrika's head in Bea's lap, dense, gray-threaded curls hidden at the base of her skull beneath the gold, like field mice in hay.

She will not tell them. It will put light in her eyes, to have a secret.

The sheep, plump in their coats, huddle in a corner pen. She tests the shears. They snap open and shut. Ulrika and August are lunching, and Bea has gone out for air. It is no lie. She cannot seem to catch a breath.

Be firm and steady of hand, August said, shear the belly first and then the legs and crotch, mindful of the teats. A task of skill, not strength. "Easy," she says to the smallest ewe. "It's only me." She grips a tuft, scissoring through close to the skin. A clean cut. What is sheared stinks of damp dog. The sheep bucks, her wool ruined by blood from one tiny, treacherous nick. Bea holds her down. How is it Nilla's prized ewe, buried by snow and the rest of the flock, ever survived on a belly full of fleece?

◊

When Bea sneaks out to the tenant cabin she finds lavender, curly dock, and chamomile hanging from the rafters, shedding buds. In the windowsill, there is a blue eggshell blown clean, a sheep skull with a spiderweb in its eye socket, a pipe spilling tobacco. The bed is unmade, the sheets unwashed, on the bedside table the purse of baby teeth. A tendril of sweet smoke rises from wood incense.

What a mess, Bea confirms with relief. Satisfied, she hurries home to the perpetual effort of beating back her own mess room by room, chore by chore.

◊

Ulrika bathes in the big house.

"Take my water," she calls to Bea. "While it's still hot."

The bathwater is lukewarm, floating with rose petals, peppermint leaves, and strands of Ulrika's hair that Bea picks from her skin.

Ulrika towels dry openly. Bea has rarely seen her sister undressed. Their differences startle—Ulrika's muscled thighs and wide hips, her long torso, stretch marks like rivulets. She has full breasts, a trail of black hair from her belly button, and Venus dimples at her low back. Bea's own breasts are pointy and small, her angles bony. If she is strong, it is because when she rubs between her legs or lies with August, she clenches from her toes to the tendons in her neck. He must have seen it, too, the slab of muscle rising from her stomach's center, like a serpent's arched back. She hugs her knees, some frailty of body and mind exposed by Ulrika's proximity. Hallucinations wake Bea nowadays from sleep heavy and dark as burial: the mattress sodden with blood that disappears in daylight, or a baby lost and mewling in the blankets.

"Beata," Ulrika begins, like she knows Bea's trouble and its remedy, but Bea slides under the scrim of suds.

◊

"Which of us is more like Angelique?" Bea demands of August. "Me or her?"

"Ulrika." He takes no time to think. "She has her spirit."

"And me?"

"You are your father's daughter."

◊

Ulrika outpaces August planting rows of wheat and corn. He fattens on her blackberry pie. At dinner they talk relentlessly of the cow's swollen udder, the ewe that three times escaped pasture, the stone wall in need of mending. Bea is no help. They protect her weak constitution. When they come home to find the fire lit, Ulrika says, "You're roasting," and throws the windows open. But when they are open to spring breeze, she says, "You'll catch a chill," poised to rub Bea's chest with goose grease and turpentine at the smallest cough. Not only August but the farmhouse seems possessed by Ulrika, daisies shivering in their vase when she props her elbows on the table, chairs creaking, ceilings lowering, grease from her lips printed on the rim of each glass. Even the sky seems lower.

When they think they are alone, Bea is watching. She is their distant, orbiting moon.

All the things she could tell him. Ulrika let boys look up her skirt. She tempted the Axelsson twin to the hayloft. Surely the villagers believe it, so why not August? There are evenings Ulrika skips dinner, when her cabin stays dark, and though Bea watches for her return, her sister never seems to come home. And where does she go, on her long walks? Three times Bea follows her, only to arrive at Bruna's hut. Still, the trailing is time to fixate on what she could find: Ulrika in the graveyard beneath the blacksmith with the wooden hand, no thought for his wife and twelve children. Or at the docks, disappearing below deck with the longshoreman, his boat swaying side to side. "Is she really the one you want?" she could demand of August. "A woman like that?"

Rage douses her, caustic as the hickory ash and rainwater Ulrika boils to make lye. She hates the sunburned length of Ulrika's neck, her chapped knuckles, her cowlicked hair. She hates how her sister turns her crimped and dim.

Ulrika doles out tincture, and Bea holds the liquid in her smiling mouth. As soon as she is alone, she spits it out.

◊

Each morning Bea wakes feeling a little less herself, as if at bedtime she brushed clean the soles of her feet and pulled up the quilt and in the night something sweet and essential siphoned from her, slowly, gradually. One day, she fears she'll be fully drained.

She tries to recall the girl she was in those months when she first knew August.

Sixteen, soft lit. In memory, her hair is tinted red, and her face is broad, peaceful, and kind. She is at home in that still-wild girl's body, always tan and sun warmed—in the field, in the hayloft, wrapping her arms around pilings at the pier, dangling her legs off the back of the cart, peeling blades of grass into smaller and smaller strips. Always it is the height of summer, insects hissing, the world beyond her limned a fresh, flickering green and August waiting just outside the frame, around each bend in the road, behind each row in the orchard, and soon, soon, he will lift her down from the apple tree, hands lingering on her hips, soon he will take out his knife and cut her a bouquet of blossoms.

◊

Her right incisor throbs with her pulse. Her tongue is coated by a starchy film. A blood vessel breaks in her eye, hairline crack in a china teacup.

In the mirror, she greets the woman from the daguerreotype: crooked features and her father's weak chin.

When was the last time August kissed her open-mouthed, hands sliding up her waist?

Now if he looks at Bea at all, it is with alarm, as if she is a specter sweeping through the room.

Who is he? Where did he go?

He is here, of course, unchanged. He has been here all along. It is Bea who is transformed.

◊

The bulbs Ulrika has planted in the kitchen garden send up shoots, and sprouts unfurl—spinach, snow peas, leeks, tufts of onion grass between the front path's flagstones. Lilacs bloom and drip rain. Bea craves dirt under her nails and weeding, the satisfying rip of loosened roots. Some can be traced back to their source, invasive nearby willow or winter creeper vine. She digs for stones, removing each wet leaf and twig. She is untroubled by centipedes, or spiders hugging their white egg sacks. By lunchtime, her dress is soil streaked and soaked at the knees, her nose running and hands numb.

When the ache starts to spread, thighs to navel to low back, she crouches and keeps tending the garden, heap of weeds and debris growing beside her, until the bed is clear. On the hillside, the sheared flock grazes. Ulrika and August are nowhere in sight. She rakes her fingers through Ulrika's sprouts. She pulls her tights to her ankles. The small, clotted shape slips out.

She will think, now and then, of the thing she buries. Or it is beneath her thoughts, in peaty darkness. Not a baby, not even close. A stone, a plum, a bulb.

*

If the bleed did not continue, she would never have told.

The flooding, Ulrika calls it, ushering Bea into her cabin. Bea drinks Ulrika's tea. Crane's-bill, yarrow, and red raspberry leaf. It turns her teeth chalky.

"Don't tell August," Bea begs from the bed. "Don't call the doctor."

"I wouldn't," Ulrika promises, curling around her. Soon, soon the bleeding stops.

"You wouldn't poison me again," Bea whispers. "Would you?"

For a long time Ulrika is quiet.

"Once, I wanted to be like Bruna. A healer," she murmurs against Bea's back. "Now in my dreams, I poison them. Those boys. Those children. They go limp. The poison spreads, house by house, like pestilence, like fire. In the dream, I regret what I've done. I try to heal them, but I don't know how." She strokes Bea's hair. "I never meant to poison you, believe me."

◊

Bea's voice echoes. The pews gleam. Empty, the church listens.

She prays for God to take away her anger and ugliness. She is uninhabitable, harsh and brittle, sour earth. She prays to be soft. Sweet. To be filled, once more, with light. To revert to the figment August pursued, before he knew her better. A girl with many colors in her hair and mismatched eyes like a pair of glittering earrings. Seen, and deemed lovely.

A boy leans against the spiked churchyard gate. He holds a bouquet of white flowers.

A long gun is slung over his shoulder.

Not a boy. Not flowers either, but a clutch of limp doves, held by their throats.

Elias stares. He stands no taller than her shoulders, in a blue velvet coat, shadows under his eyes and pockmarks dotting his cheeks as if he's leaned into a spray of sparks.

"Supper?" she asks, nodding as she passes by.

"Still life," he says.

Part V

The animal carving hides at the back of Bea's bedside drawer. She has not held it in years. The wood is gray, light as a bone. She rubs her thumb along the smooth ridges of the ears, the haunches, the hollows of its eyes and mouth.

She has been thinking lately of wolves, drawn inexplicably from mainland to island. She feels them closing in, but other times she is with them in the waves, paddling through chop and white spray, breath chuffing, legs churning.

◊

The storage room at the back of the grocer smells of sawdust and rot. Here, she learned that Mikael beat his children senseless with the slat of an onion crate, Lars ravished young Maia after last year's spring dance, Maia brought the carnal act upon herself by drinking too much bilberry mead then went to Bruna for an abortifacient, and Boe branded his initials into his heifer's ears when his wife ran off with the neighboring cowherd. She overheard news of

185

herself—how she shuffled to town in her nightgown with the top buttons undone. The truth about her stretched, like the store's scant inventory of flour mixed with plaster. She was a drunk or brainsick. The story abated, in time. At least people stopped staring.

All her life, she's waited on talk of her mother. When in hushed tones they said, "That girl never knew what was good for her" then quieted, she allowed her mother to be that girl, turning the words over in her mind like a code.

Now Ada, Katrine, and Vera gossip with the grocer's daughter, Frida.

They say Elias is home because he worked himself ill, writing poems soon to be published on the mainland. He lives on cardamom buns and white wine. "And opium," whispers Ada. "And Erik suspects he's paid well for companionship," adds Katrine. At the tavern, he fell asleep on the beer-sticky back bench. Bruna helped him home but not before he broke a bottle of brännvin at the neck. Katrine, swollen with Erik Axelsson's fourth child, is frightened to share a house with him. Entering his wing, she hears moaning.

Bea feels an upswelling of the old urge to parse his looks. Instead, she digs her fingers into the acrid bin of coffee beans, picking out counterfeits—roasted peas and pebbles in her fist. Ada reminds them how her wrist aches each time it rains. "Don't forget, he attacked me. We might drive him out," she says. "An odd man like that, around our children." Ada's two girls careen around the corner and gape at Bea, the smaller one unfolding a strand of yellowed paper dolls.

◊

She takes a trampled path to the shore, sidestepping scat threaded with hair. The sand is back.

Every year, at the autumnal equinox, strong tides carry the sand away. All winter, the beach is bare dark stones, easy to twist an ankle. Bea can look down from the North Cliffs to the sandbar's pale submerged shape, winding through the bay like a leviathan, grounding ships. The oldest villagers recall a time when the sand disappeared for decades. Then like magic, after a spring full of storms, it returned overnight.

Already thin strands of dune grass grow. Blown by wind, they scratch faint concentric circles in the sand, like ripples in a pond or the growth rings of an oak. When she was little the shapes were signs, even after Ulrika pointed out the blade of grass at each center.

Sand wolf spiders crawl back into their silk-lined holes. Crabs skitter. Bea picks a distant boulder. When she reaches it, she lays her hand to its coarse-grained warmth in greeting.

Sometimes, the island itself is there for her.

Elias is sitting by the estuary.

She can avoid no one if she is to leave the house. She continues toward him on her slim patch of sand, slipping off her shoes, watching the water like he's the last thing on her mind.

There is something inside her Elias of all people might detect—loneliness or want, shame or wickedness, changeable and raw—the same unspoken, ill-concealed signal that beckons the woman to Bea's window. Or maybe the whole village can detect it. Now when she goes out, buttoned up and neat in her apron and kerchief, it is hard to shake the sensation of undress, that despite her best efforts she is still shuffling along in her nightgown.

He looks up from his book. The breeze musses his hair.

"Hello," he calls. "Amanda."

Bea knows no Amanda. He mistakes her, so he stares. That is all.

"You're a vision," he says.

It is too late to turn back. He is smiling like they share a secret.

"Beata," she corrects him. Inescapable.

"Don't," he says, voice deep and gravelly. "I'm on the twenty-third sonnet. For you. One for each day since the churchyard." His eyes shiver left to right, their pupils tiny.

"Have I changed so much?" she asks. "Surely you remember. Beata. Ulrika's sister."

"I couldn't forget." A shroud of tiny, biting black flies surrounds them, drawn by their stillness. "Please." Elias flips open the notebook, fingers shaking and ink stained.

"You're no mere Beata. I just finished a new sonnet this morning. I'm writing one now in my head."

His elegant handwriting has turned barely decipherable, marked by the whorls of his fingerprints.

"Look to your Latin," he says. "Amanda. She who is worthy of love."

◊

She finds the poems at the end of her drive, tucked in the hollow of the wide-crowned oak where he promised to leave them. He makes quick work. Each day, a new poem.

She holds the tiny scroll between two fingers, touching its tip to her mouth.

Back in bed, she smooths out "Amanda Sonnet 36."

Amanda's favorite season is springtime. She pulls off her cap and shakes out her hair. Her eyes gleam the gold of childhood meadows. Her body is like a dogwood, scented, pink blooming.

In one poem she wears a crown of lilies, in another a crown of snow, a crown of nettles.

She is sunlight and grape must and loam, close as his breath on the pillow, distant as the morning star.

She dreams blue. Soaks and swims in oceans, rivers, lakes, and streams, nymphlike. She rises from the incoming tide. She wears a dress of ivy. A dress of fire.

Bea has never put her fingers inside herself. She reaches up her nightgown. She eases her way in. She has imagined

189

what she finds will be smooth as the inside of her cheek, but instead it is rough like the roof of her mouth, like walnut shell. Elias's voice is in her ear, his exact timbre and pacing, a low urgent rumble. Her hips rock. Her hand is wet.

Knuckles rap the door.

She stops when August comes in. Her hand smells elemental, tidal. Panicked, she puts her fingers in her mouth.

He is here to try again. They are still trying, rarely and shyly, touch tentative and halting like a second language too long unspoken. She fumbles with his buttons. They knock teeth. "You feel good," she says. "I feel so good." She mouths the name Elias, softly, only once.

"Bless our baby," says August, kissing her stomach when at last she feels the quickening. "Bless our house." He tucks blankets around Bea's legs. Ulrika brushes Bea's hair, sparking static. They lay her fires, bring basins of steaming water to soak her swollen feet. Mornings, August delivers her blue-green eggs and Ulrika fries them, fresh yolks the color of the woodland's marsh marigolds. Toast arrives with its acorn-shaped butter. If she tucks the animal carving beneath her pillow, her sleep is tranquil as a bowl of warm milk. Her cravings are constant. While August and Ulrika dig furrows in the field she shoots three doves—marveling at her fine aim—and roasts them on a spit, picking the bones clean of gamy meat with her teeth. She eats snow pea pods by the fistful. In her fifth month, Ulrika lets out Bea's waistbands. Her footfalls shake the stairs. She does not creep through the house, invisible. She stomps. Her skin shines. Even the creases of her eyelids are oily, temples gleaming. As in pubescence, she rubs gray beach stones on her face to polish them black. "Little frogs," she sings, "no ears, no ears, no tails have they." Undressing to bathe, she cannot see between her legs. A dark line bisects the length of her belly; she takes this as a sign she will give August a son. For

ANNA NOYES

the first time, she has breasts, she has heft. *Amanda*. The
private renaming works on her like the word *woman*, like
wife, like *mother*, lighting her up. Her breath comes quick
and shallow. Her body thrums with pleasure and warning.
Best to tuck herself back into a small shape. But she feels
on the cusp of something, arms flung open. A precipice
with a steep drop. Alarming joy. A smile, growing wider
and wider and wider across her face.

◊

She sits with her back against the door. She is meant to
be dressing for church. She lifts her skirt, spreads her legs.
Something is amiss, tingling verging on burning.

When she lies down to nap, instead of sleeping she
touches herself and thinks of Elias. Of his strange face
and how he watches her—eyeglass lenses fogging like she
is a poem incarnate—but mainly of his voice. She can
conjure it anytime she needs, though afterward cannot
recall what was said, only his measured, scratchy rhythm,
steady as a purr.

Now she feels blighted, swollen.

She holds up the hand mirror. She had never seen
this part of her.

There is no bat, no spider.

It is the purple of a bruise, rimmed with soft brown
hair. Hot to the touch.

◊

Already, this year, God has flooded the barley and infected the cattle with mange. "Make no mistake," the new priest tells them, "God punishes only as any loving parent must. He comes for what we cherish so we can wake up. So we can right the ship." He is older than her father lived to be, cheeks latticed by broken blood vessels. Elias eyes her from his post at the church doors, where he stands during sermons like a sentry in his velvet coat.

She feels her soul withdrawing from God, deeded to darkness with each unrepented urge.

She prays, then, for August to be well, tipping her head to his shoulder. No matter that visions edge in of life without him, vague and spacious. The bow of a boat. Wind in her hair.

Harm me, the prayer unfolds as she kneels. *If You must, punish me.* A second thought rises, smoke from a snuffed candle: *If You must, take the baby.* This, she cannot claim. It is the Devil sweeping through her, then up into the rafters and out over the fallow fields and lowing cattle toward the sea.

"Oh day full of grace," she stands to sing. "Oh good day full of grace, full of grace."

◊

The thing inside her flips and squirms. It was conceived— she understands—when she called August by Elias's name. He had not noticed. She cordons off thoughts of her fifteen-year-old self, blanket tight over her head,

193

convinced the Devil wended his way in through her body's apertures. She wants to be good. She does not go to Elias's door in a nightgown and slippers wet with slush. She stops touching herself and repeats, *Lord keep me from Satan and sin.* But she cannot stop reading the poems.

And one fantasy reoccurs: her naked body in the barn—where she hid with the horses while her sister was stitched—seen from outside herself and from behind, bent over the stable's gate. Elias is nowhere in the vision. She does not know who she waits for.

◊

The church bells ring at dawn, after a night of snow and lightning. Someone has spotted smoke. Clanging carries across the island. The canon overlooking the harbor blasts once, twice, summoning everyone, even Bea, who nine months pregnant struggles to draw breath. The ride to town bundled between August and Ulrika is gentle, sleigh runners shushing, pines and lanes and rooftops smoothed by snow.

Fire rages neatly inside the barn. Its walls are perfectly intact, and it looks as if it might be saved, despite the billowing smoke, though there is nothing to see through the barn's windows but flames. For once, August and Ulrika are too troubled to tell her not to trouble herself. She hurries as best she can to fill her bucket at the springhouse, then like the rest of the villagers splashes her small offering of water. The barn burns too hot to get close. The flames sound like a cyclone. Above the roar she hears the horses screaming, trapped inside.

Farmer Lofgren runs into the barn to save them.

"Get back," shouts Lars. "The haybales are catching."

The islanders form a distant ring to watch. Ash floats down with snow.

Elias takes notes as the roof caves.

In church for Farmer Lofgren's funeral, the priest will remind them of God's displeasure but also of His mercy. A dry day, a windy day, an arid season, or a lightning strike in summer and things could have gone differently, the fire spreading to the nearby church, the celebration hall, the springhouse, the gristmill, the schoolhouse, their homesteads, one by one.

"Heed His warning," he continues. "Does it please Him, when you dance yourselves to ruin? When your girls wear colored ribbons and your boys drag sticks along my churchyard fence? Open your eyes. I fear I got here just in time. Charlock is overtaking the barley and the bread has turned bitter."

Bea spots Ulrika straddling the branch of a tree at the edge of the alvar. She walks to the base of the trunk. Her breath hangs white in the air.

"What are you doing up there?"

"Guarding the rooks," Ulrika says, though the nests were abandoned years ago, when farmers blamed the rooks, not God, for a season of failed crops and gored lambs. Their schoolmates used to climb the rookery trees to net and kill birds returning to their nests at night. Bea and Ulrika hunkered in the branches as protectors, but those rooks left on the island moved into the woods. "You wouldn't be up there," Lars had said, kicking the base of the trunk, "if your father was a farmer." The abandoned nests were threaded through with hair, scraps of ribbon, sewing thread, moss, straw, and bast. In some, fledglings peeped, and Bea and Ulrika brought them worms.

Ulrika jumps down and loops her arm around Bea, hand resting on Bea's swollen belly. Their hair is flecked with ash, their faces soot streaked. Ulrika wipes her cheeks with the fringe of her shawl but cannot seem to stop crying.

"I know what will cheer you," Ulrika says at last, like Bea is the one who needs comforting. She pats her coat pockets. "I'm someone's muse," she says. "Can you imagine?" She pulls out a curled paper. "That funny little Elias writes me poems. 'Our secret,' he told me, like he was changing my life. Not even a smile? Read it. He calls me Amanda."

Bea finds the hen that lays Ulrika's favorite blue-green eggs snug in its roost. She snaps its neck.

The crunch of Ulrika's footsteps follows her to the water, impossible to outpace. "Can't I have one scrap?"

Bea says. "Just one, to myself?" Bea cannot tell where the beach ends and the frozen bay begins, under its blanket of snow. She trudges out, the baby kicking inside her.

"Wait," shouts Ulrika, but she'll keep going, for as long as she can, right up to the floe edge.

She plunges in, and sinks.

The current yanks her skirt. Her boots are heavy. If she could open her mouth, cold would shock a scream from her. But she keeps her mouth closed and opens her eyes underwater. She rises. She has always been buoyant. Ulrika used to dive off the dock and down for treasure— oarlock, flask, coin, brooch—but when Bea tried she could never reach the bay's cloudy depth, fingers straining toward shapes socketed in soft muck as she floated back up.

She mistakes the underside of the ice for the sky.

She knocks. She batters. When she swims, her animal self knows the right direction because she surfaces, gasping, clawing at the lip of ice to lift herself. Someone is screaming. Ulrika pulls Bea from the water. For one moment they breathe, foreheads together, before Ulrika stoops to carry her. "I've got you," she says as she begins to run.

"Get Bruna," Ulrika shouts to August. "I won't leave her."

But the doctor arrives with his big black bag. He reaches in, up to the elbow.

"Is the baby alright?" August asks. "Will it live?"

"You Silasdotter girls are reckless," says the doctor. "Just like your mother."

Bea is numb and shaking but feels wondrous, wide awake. The baby hiccoughs inside her. Her soaked dress, draped on the chair like a guest, drips. There is blood under her nails, the tenderness before a bruise across her knuckles. Everywhere, flickers of pain. The doctor presses his stethoscope to her stomach. It is shaped like a trumpet.

"The baby's coming," she tells them.

◊

Ulrika holds Bea between her thighs. "Stay," Bea says, and Ulrika says, "Always." Bea leans back against Ulrika's chest and feels her heart pound. When the doctor tells Ulrika to leave the bed, Bea growls. They are slick with sweat. When Bea's legs shake, Ulrika's do, her skin gouged with purple crescents from Bea's clutching. Bea wants to climb out of herself. When she howls, Ulrika does, the pain shared but not halved. August pokes his head around the door. Bea tightens her hold on Ulrika's hand. "You are mine," she tells her sister. "He cannot have you."

"And you are mine," Ulrika says.

Bea hears herself plead, "When will the labor begin? Is this labor? Has it begun?" And when she cannot speak, only gnash her teeth and bear down and rock her hips, she is still thinking, *When, when, when?*

The doctor, poised at the foot of the bed, recoils.

199

A gray-pink sac balloons between her legs. With a final push, it slews out. It breaks open. The water drains. Her son draws his first breath.

They place him to her chest. He grips her finger tight. "Hold on," she says. Of course, he is not cloven-footed. Two faces do not crowd his skull. He bears no sign of her sin, that bottomless want.

But the field outside her window morphs, eddying silver grass and black boulders. Always nighttime. Her nightgown sours. Her nipples scab. There is blood in the milk.

Alone with the baby, she lets him cry and lie there soiled, but she is not herself. Ulrika sweeps in, scoops him up. It should be morning soon. Bea cups the baby's heavy head. But no, it's August's mouth. Milk flows at the slightest touch. How nice it is to be drained. "Not as sweet as you'd think," he says, lips to her skin. The baby snuffles in his crib, hungry again. She is a wellspring.

The lambs cry all hours. She is a salt lick. A horse drapes her with its soft mane. It licks and licks her with a rough tongue. She cannot sleep. Ulrika waits at the bedside, putting out heat. Refusing to leave, stoking a fire under her skirt. She takes the baby from Bea's chest. "Lucky boy," she croons, unbuttoning her blouse. "Born en caul so he won't drown, will he?" She has no milk, still he suckles.

"But he's mine," Bea says.

"Lucky boy." Ulrika rocks him. "Sees the past and the future."

The boy reveals himself as ugly. Hands dry and grasping. Irises leaking their green into a distended belly. Drip by drip, until there's nothing left but pupils, and they trail her. She puts things inside herself where the baby was. Dishcloths and ice. She is loose and ragged. She does not know if she'll heal.

Blue dust covers every surface. Her mouth is packed with wool and gnats sip at her eyes.

The witch waits at the window. Her long arms trail the ground. Bea rises to pass the baby over, so the woman may wrap her arms around and around him, as a spider mummifies the source of tremors in her web.

"Hold on," Ulrika says. "I'll hurry back." While she is gone, the doctor returns. "Excuse her indecency," says August.

"She knows no better," answers the doctor. "Puerperal insanity. It's not uncommon." He struggles Bea into a tepid bath, forcing her to drink from his medicine bottle, rust-colored droplets pluming in the water. There is no more struggle then, and she floats, languid. "Not to worry," the doctor tells August, "Her halo of love is returning already." And she can sense the radiance surrounding her, like candlelight around a flame. But when she wakes to find the baby gone and her wrists tied, she calls them both the worst names she can summon.

"You must eat," August says, prodding Bea's lips with tines. The fork needles its way in.

When Bruna arrives with her basket of herbs, she unties one wrist and Ulrika the other. The room is sealed up tight and grows warm as any bath, and Bea's hands are held and stroked, and the baby returned to her chest.

"Your sister took good care of you," says Bruna. "You are doing so well."

Bea squeezes Ulrika's hand. "How did our mother die?"

"You know how."

"Tell me," Bea pleads. "Just tell me. Tell me."

"I remember the day you were born," Ulrika says.

It's as if Bea remembers, too.

The doctor laid Bea on her mother's chest and stitched her. Smiling, she touched Bea's tiny ears and lips and fingers.

Later. Nighttime.

"I'm watching from her doorway," says Ulrika. "The sound that drew me, silenced. Somewhere, you are crying. Silas stands over her bed. He doesn't see me. I am a spirit."

Something's wrong, she tells him. *Get Bruna.*

Ulrika's not mine, he says, rocking back and forth. *I saw when I held Beata. Ulrika's his.*

I'm bleeding, she answers. *Too much.*

You are out of control, he says. *My wife.*

I'm bleeding.

Yes.

"He prays for her. Forgives her. Her eyes find mine, over his shoulder. *Run*, she tells me. Time slows. Her face drains of color. He does not move. I do not move."

Run.

Run.

"When I finally do, I am afraid," Ulrika says. "I run and hide under my bed."

◊

Bea sleeps. Wakes.

The baby cries and quiets when she lifts him. He knows her voice. She kisses the soft crown of his head. He burrows at her neck. Her boy.

She has been brainsick, surely, but like a fever it has broken. Ulrika is there. Bruna is there. She sips their pond-water tea, picking at Ulrika's platter of seared trout, collecting bones in her cheek. Bruna combs and braids Bea's matted hair. Now the window is cracked open. The sunlight catches dust motes. On the breeze, spring thaw. She had thought she would die, but she is alive.

The baby has August's bowed upper lip.

It is time he has a name.

They'll call him August and Auggie for short.

With each passing moment, he looks more his father's son, big ears, worried brow.

Bea stares at Ulrika, as if for the first time. Her sister has August's jaw, his long neck, his height, and his hands.

Her surprise is like a far-off flash of lightning. As a girl, she counted seconds between lightning and thunder, gauging her distance from the storm. The counting soothed.

1-2-3-4-5.

"Leave us," she tells Ulrika and Bruna.

6-7-8-9-10.

August joins her in the bed, the baby between them. He kisses the bruise on her knuckles.

"Is Ulrika yours?" Bea asks.

"Mine?"

She traces the baby's spiraling cowlick.

"Your daughter."

For a long time, he says nothing. Then his shoulders sag. "I don't know. Silas suspected so. I promised him my silence."

His story unfolds in a soft voice so the baby won't wake.

It was Angelique's idea, to steal the horse from Lofgren's barn. She caught him in the dark outside the celebration hall, whispering into his ear, *Escape with me?* He was dizzy drunk, hilarity and pleasure that would end in sickness. She was already engaged to the priest, an arrangement to make her pious mother and God happy. So happy, Angelique hoped, that maybe she would live. Angelique was grieving.

They galloped the spotted mare through the woods to the pier. No one watched them board his uncle's boat. The prow sliced through calm dark water. On the Blue Maiden's shore, alone at last, they undressed. He had never seen a woman down to her slip. Limbs wine heavy, he imitated stuttering Silas, asking Angelique for a stroll after church.

"Don't be cruel," she scolded, wading into the bay. Why choose a man twenty years their senior, whom she did not love? "Do you imagine I love you?" she smiled, trailing phosphorescence, green blinkering in the black. "I love the island," she said. "But he is kind and steady. And pleased enough I know how he takes his tea."

"I am kind," replied August. "I am steady." He staggered against the surf.

In the water, she wrapped her legs loosely around his hips, her floating body weightless. He had never been with a woman before.

He would not lie with another, until Bea.

"I loved her recklessly," he says. "I'm sorry. I've told you too little, now I've told you too much."

At dawn, they dressed. She picked a white stone from the Blue Maiden's beach and slipped it into her pocket. "To remember you by." Their hair still damp, she rowed them back to Berggrund.

Silas waited on the dock, in his priest's robe.

He helped her from the boat. "Wherever you've been," he said, "whatever you've done, come with me. Confess. Be forgiven."

"I was not a kind man," August says, "but a resentful one. I didn't speak to her again. Not even when her mother died. I left. I didn't open her letters."

Last he saw Angelique, she sat alone on the beach, burying her long legs in the sand. She mounded sand over her stomach, wet and dark. It was her wedding night. He wished she would bury herself to the neck and then bury her head.

Instead she burst free and ran, diving headfirst into a wave just as it broke.

Nine months later, Ulrika was born.

◊

Bea is supposed to stay inside. Instead, she joins her sister on the stoop.

Ulrika's eyes are wild, as if she's just given birth, as if she's woken from a delirium, too. She wears her long, dark coat, draws on her pipe.

"You came back to me," Ulrika says. "I was terrified to lose you."

Bea scans Ulrika's face for something definite. Proof. Words gather force inside her and a crackling rage. *We're not even full sisters*, she could say. *You're a bastard*. Like she's spoken aloud, her anger is mirrored in Ulrika's eyes. Bea deems their mother its source. Viking blood that could burn the whole village to the very ground.

"I was not supposed to be there, when you were born," Ulrika says. "I crept up on the doctor to watch over his shoulder. Your head appeared, then with your body still inside her, you opened your eyes. My sister." She takes Bea's hand, fingernails gnawed to the quick. "For

207

years, I remembered his moaning, his wet face. 'What happened?' he whined when the doctor came. 'What did I do?' The doctor said she'd hemorrhaged. The village women cleaned her, scrubbing the stain from the mattress. They put a candle in her hands. I lit the wick.

"I blamed you," Ulrika says. "I hated you. Then I learned to feed you and change you and stop your crying. Those things looked like loving. In time, I did. I do. But the voice in my ear still tells me to run."

They hold each other's gaze.

"I used to think Father's death would change things," Ulrika says. "And I'd be free."

They lean against each other. "You're free now," says Bea. The terror of losing Ulrika twines with the hope of becoming herself. Ulrika exhales a stream of smoke.

"I thought you loved August," Bea says. "Why else live here? Why stay so long?"

"I stayed for you." Ulrika taps clean her pipe. "You really have no idea who I am," she says, though not unkindly. "Or who I love."

For six weeks, Bea does not leave her bedroom.

New mothers isolate to rejuvenate, the priest assures, not because they are impure. Still, she is not welcome in the village or at the table with her family. She cannot share the cutlery. She eats with Auggie, in her bed. "Keep your strength," Ulrika says, dropping off cream-rich puddings at Bea's door. She drags a rocker into the hall. When Bea hears the creak of its runners, she does not know if her sister guards as protector or captor. August rarely crosses the room's threshold. Now she's tethered to the baby, and the thread connecting her to August slackens. He carries their son away, then brings him back, christened. Village women descend on the farm, as if there has been a death. They cook and clean, avoiding Bea like her presence pollutes the air. Despite what the priest says, islanders understand an old truth, that a mother before her churching ceremony is dirty and dangerous. As good as unbaptized.

Just as well.

For six weeks, she gets to stay beneath the covers, her arms around her son.

Real dangers lurk everywhere, present and pressing. Even clean, crisp sheets give him a rash. Beyond

ANNA NOYES

the bedroom's four walls wait steaming kettles, rattling coughs, serrated blades, stomping footfalls, errant wasps, poisonous leaves he will try to grip in his sweaty fist, unbreakable curses. Worse. Chaos, as her father would say. A story they are all born into.

How does anyone mother?

Giving birth, she became animal, if not impure. The wooden spoon Ulrika forced into her mouth so she might bite down bears her teeth marks, and a crack through its center. Now she knows the force that sleeps inside her. Need be, she suspects she can summon that ferocious, surging strength again, to keep them both safe.

But the question won't stop haunting her: How? How is anyone brave enough? How, island women with twelve children, three of whom live to see their fourth birthday? How, when her son is endlessly hungry for her, and her own desire is insatiable? How to survive?

If Bea is caught, she can say she sleepwalks. But she is wide awake, lacing her boots and belting a coat over her nightgown, swaddling Auggie in his crib and creeping past Ulrika snoring in her rocker.

Outside, she can breathe. The tree frogs are churring.

She walks the long length of the island alone, corn crake croaking like a clock wound tighter and tighter. At the priest's house, shadows move behind the curtain of

210

the third-story window. She kneels in the garden. She knows just where to dig and will rip up the entire bed if she must, each neat row of hyacinth, spraying dirt behind her like Helmi after a buried bone.

The Blue Maiden stone is small and cold, covered in soil. She wipes it clean. New motherhood has been all instinct. Retrieve the stone and the red book. Do not abide another minute shut up in your room.

Elias's house is unlocked, all windows dark but one. Her footsteps echo down the long hall. The clock chimes three.

When she imagined knocking at Elias's door, dressed in black silk stockings and flushed from the bath, it was often August who answered, and he knelt, pressing his cheek to her stomach, and she held him there tightly.

Elias's door is open. He lies on his back, legs hanging off the side of the bed, boots soaked through as if he just stumbled home from the tavern. Books and papers crowd him. He has a black eye, a swollen lip.

"You're here," he says.

"I saw your light."

"You look like you've escaped the grave," he says. "Are you alright?"

Her nightgown is muddy, hair lank, arms dirty to her elbows and her pockets heavy with talismans, like her girlhood self has been unearthed. *Heathen*, her father called her.

"I could ask you the same."

"I've never been well liked," he answers.

In their wet clothes, both are shivering.

She kneels and pulls off his boots. He lets her ease him from his overcoat. His shoulder blades are sharp through his dress shirt.

"Were the poems ever about me?"

He looks at her carefully, closely. "No," he says. "Per-haps parts of you. The first one was." He closes his eyes. "I think I'll only meet my Amanda when I die. Soulmates, united. It's harder to love down here." He smiles. "Imagine what raspberries taste like in heaven."

"Why did you come home?" she asks. "Wasn't the mainland better?"

"This place pulled me back. I've never found another as quiet, where the streets are as dark or the stars as bright."

He opens the locket tucked in his collar, shaking blue pills into his palm and swallowing them without water.

"And I'm afraid I'm in some pain. These help," he says, offering one.

But her night isn't over yet, and she must get home to her boy.

She pulls the animal carving from her pocket and asks if he will consider another trade.

"That carving is protective," he tells her. "Keep it."

He points to the red book on the shelf, though of course she has seen it already. It catches the eye like a cardinal in snow.

"It's yours. Beata," he sighs, "would you stay with me until I fall asleep? The medicine is quick."

She tucks the quilt around him. She kisses his cheek. She wishes she could say she is sorry.

Outside the church, she imagines throwing the stone through its arched window, Mary and Joseph with their babe in the hay. But even to think it hurts.

The church is open.

Something, someone inside is listening, the air alive.

Even in nighttime, she feels the slant of warm light through stained glass, and her breathing slows, and her shoulders soften. She dips her fingers into the tepid water of the baptismal font and showers her face with droplets. She stands where the priest stands, and she absolves herself.

When she lies down in the pew, for the first time in weeks she sleeps well enough to dream. She walks the grassland. People throw fruit at men in pillories. People eat meat shaved from a sow. Someone grabs her from behind and holds a knife to her throat. She cannot twist to see their face.

"Please," she begs, "I am a daughter. I am a sister." They hold her tightly. "I am a wife, a mother," she says. "Beata. My name is Beata."

The blade is quick.

Laid out on her back, the sky is filled with stars and her body with light that consumes and lifts her up, up, like sparks rising.

At dawn, Bea picks a poppy, its petals just opening. She is not quite ready to go back inside.

When she does, Ulrika's rocker is empty, creaking gently back and forth. Across the field, her sister sits in the cabin window. Bea settles at the desk by her own window. Now and then she glances up, but their eyes never meet.

Bea writes as Auggie nurses, the first of her own sonnets.

The poppy's outsized shadow wavers on the wall, the candle melts into a pool of wax, the porridge left outside her door grows cold, petals droop, the baby sleeps, wakes, an ant crawls across her knuckles. Today, this is how she survives.

◊

"The Lord is my light and salvation," the new priest begins, "whom shall I fear? The Lord is the stronghold of my life, of whom shall I be afraid?" Bea walks the aisle. Before her, the island's girls fan themselves with branches cut from the linden tree. Behind her, the mothers process, draped in long wool shawls despite the heat, children jostling on their hips. Bea kneels on the plush

pillow as the priest murmurers benediction above her.
She kisses his hand, and he pats her head. "Welcome
back to us, dear girl."

After the churching ceremony, though light rain has been
falling for days, her small, shifting family takes her to the
shore. Their footsteps make shallow pools in the newly
returned sand.

"Swim with me?" asks Ulrika.

Perhaps it is the cool of the rain, but the water feels
oddly warm, lapping her ankles. They undress to their
slips. When she passes her son to August, he stoops to kiss
her, and though they have not touched in six weeks her
breasts let down their milk.

"Look," he says, turning Auggie to face the waves.
The breeze flutters her baby's hair, fine as milkweed floss.
"Off they go."

She follows Ulrika into the water, ripples all around
them.

The bay is the color of the sky, the Blue Maiden hidden by mist, the expanse stretching on and on.

They submerge together.

Bea opens her eyes, and Ulrika is looking back. For
a moment, they belong only to each other. Sisters. Alone.
They take hands. Their hair undulates, the gold-red of
algae that drapes the rocks and sunken ships and the hulls
of boats safe in the harbor.

*

In the morning, Ulrika is gone.

Bea finds the briefest note in her cabin: *I am sorry. I had to. I love you.*

She does not believe what the empty drawers tell her. The embers still glow in the cookstove. The kettle is full.

For the rest of her long life, Bea will sink down into the pause with Ulrika underwater—how quiet and clear and gentle it was—before the surface started simmering.

They rose into a deluge, the storm broken. They tipped their heads back and filled their mouths with rain.

◊

Bea sees Ulrika's future as if she lives it.

A boat's deck empty of passengers. She walks its circular route. The night air cools her scalp, shaved bare for the lice, with a razor she keeps beneath her pillow. The nausea that gripped her after departure has finally subsided. They have reached open ocean, no sight of land in all directions. Spray cools her sunburned arms. Gulls coast in the ship's draft, still begging for scraps so many miles offshore. At the stern, a ribbon of white, churning water unspools. She watches the wake.

Part VI

Auggie grows up frightened of everything that frightens Bea—and more.

Eels. Veins. Sleep. Rogue waves. Gristle in meat. Rooks swooping to guard their nests. Bea's daguerreotype portrait on the mantle. "You?" he demands as soon as he can talk, distraught. "You? Mama? Mama?"

When he can walk, he follows her everywhere—hugging her legs, trying to scale her. His elbows and heels dig into her belly, soft from carrying him inside her. August names him the Shadow. If she sneaks away, his distant cry—piercing as a catbird call—accompanies each harried second on the chamber pot.

On the surface, motherhood is bravery, the part of her that is scared forced dormant. Her arms grow lean and muscled from carrying his dense little body.

She hooks two fingers down his throat and scoops free the button as he bites her.

She steps between him and the snarling dog.

She is quick, keen, sharp as flint.

*

But he does not feel safe.

Of course, he is her shadow.

And she has never felt safe.

There was always the doctor opening his black bag, the knife whittling away at the rotten stump.

If only she could hide herself from him. Even in infancy, he seemed tuned to each miniscule shift in her breathing, heartbeat, temperature, and tone. On mornings she smiles until her cheeks ache, he will ask over and over, "What is wrong?"

She thinks of the woman outside desperate to get in, pressed against glass, her features distorted.

◊

She tries to store each sweetness inside her.

August strings a hammock between two oaks. He swings with Auggie asleep on his chest. Together, her son is tiny and August enormous, broad hands cupping the boy's back. He rises and falls on his father's breath as the wind rocks them.

◊

In the barn, they watch the ewe birth, August's arms streaked with blood, as they are during spring slaughter. "Someday, this will be your job," he says to Auggie afterward. The ewe licks the lamb until it unfolds its legs.

220

They look out over the field and fences, the alvar stretching beyond. "Someday, you will own all this."

◊

When he is three years old, she wakes to his screams, coming from the nursery.

She finds him crouched against his headboard.

"A rabbit," he gasps, pointing to the ceiling. "A skinned rabbit."

◊

Before bed he begins begging for stories, clinging like she is a raft. He finds something to fear in the mildest ones, as if he craves the feeling, as she once did. She cannot tell him the stories she knows. She is too tired to invent new ones. The sheet twists around him, his arms thrown wide as if he is falling.

Soon, before someone else does, she will have to tell him a version of the island's story. Women flying off with children, dancing on Blockula, labyrinths walked forever. His eyes will light with recognition, like the witch has come for him already. Now and then, Bea has an inkling that Blockula is confined neither to legend nor the Blue Maiden, but is all around them, a realm they cannot escape or wake from.

"Long, long ago," she wants to begin, "this village was different. Nothing like it is today."

The story can be told in different ways and warn of different things, but the ending is always the same.

◊

And now he is four, and she runs to his room, and he is shouting, "I know what happened to you."

For a moment, she thinks he speaks to her.

"Just a dream," she says, holding him.

He points to the ceiling where the skinned rabbit once hovered. "There were women. Without hair. Without skin."

She knows what they must look like.

"What happened?"

"I'm awake now," he says. "I can't remember."

For a long time, they are quiet. She lies in bed beside him. "Flip onto your belly," she finally says. "Here's how we'll get to sleep." She turns over with him. "You're riding the back of an animal. Giant, and slow. It will carry you away."

It seems he needs no help to see it or sense the sway of its gait.

"Can you feel it breathing?"

At night, her husband and son asleep at last in their separate rooms, Bea returns to the red book.

It is written in many different hands. Her mother's botanical drawings are meticulous and tame.

In the earliest pages, she deciphers the nearly illegible scrawl:

To gain the strength of 5 men: Grind the root of Artemisia vulgaris with saffron and smear it across your skin.

So a virgin will not get pregnant: Dissolve shavings from the church bell, mercury, ground glass, and bone dust in a beer and make her drink.

To take power from your enemies: Bind three sprigs of hemlock with string dyed red by hare's blood. Drop this on their doorstep. They will lose all will and strength.

Bea shuts her eyes but cannot force the book's curiosities out of mind—faded sketches of women leading starbursts of light around on leashes. Wading in a long procession into the ocean. Maddening drawings of hybrid

223

plants—roots of one, leaves of another, bloom of a third—that do not exist. Sentences written in red ink, unreadable language. Half-asleep, she speaks its tongue.

She wakes to the sound of Ulrika's laughter. *She's here, she's back, at last.* It is only the wind.

◊

When Auggie begs for a bedtime story, Bea brings him the book.

He lays his head on her chest. She wonders if he feels her heart pounding.

She inscribes her name, then helps her son sign *August* in his crooked writing. He is just learning his letters. Together, they sound out her mother's name, her sister's name.

"Amen," she says, and he echoes, "Amen."

At the jagged edge of each torn page, he asks, "What was here?"

"What do you think?"

She does not tell him how she watched it happen, loose pages floating on the estuary's current.

◊

Bruna offers Bea and Auggie bowls of tiny wild strawberries and seats beside the fire.

The berries are sweet and red all the way to the stem.

"When I was your age," Bruna tells Auggie, "strawberries grew all over this island. Each Sunday, my grandmother and I made tarts. Now I'm lucky to pick one handful."

"What happened?" Auggie rolls glossy berries around the bottom of the bowl like he is panning for gems.

"Storms, draughts. Farming, grazing. Terrible winters. Sometimes in spring things don't come back." She smiles. "Last year, the swans. But on this morning's walk, paddling in the shallows, two of them."

◊

The three of them walk the alvar. They find what Angelique and Ulrika found. Tangles of whitewater crowfoot floating on the bog and windflower blanketing the forest floor each May. St. Peter's keys sprouting from cracks in the alvar's rock, where it looks like nothing should grow. Lady of the Snows pasques, said to bloom where blood spilled.

"You know, your mother thought to leave once, too," says Bruna, squinting into the sun. "But your father discovered her packed bag. The only sign was her dresses back on their hangers. By then, you were a seed inside her. Better to stay, she decided." She scuffs bare limestone with her boot. "Your sister asked me to go with her." Her eyes well. "I told her I was needed here. That life was no different, someplace else."

They enter the woods, Auggie looking back and forth from his grandmother's drawing of a pitcher plant to the real thing, filled to the brim with gnats and rain.

Bruna's crooked hands peel a strip of pine bark back to the soft, sweet sapwood. "It's good," she promises, feeding Auggie a piece.

"I do miss her," Bruna says. "Ulrika."

Once Bea sees Ulrika and Bruna's love, it is everywhere.

◊

The island offers itself to Bea in crystalline glimpses: ant trundling with its leaf, lichen that smells of violets, pink flare of rosa rugosa. She shivers, gouging the soft petals with her fingernails, slipping some into her pocket. Her bare feet waver in the rippling water of the tide pool.

When they meet Elias near the estuary, he asks what Auggie is looking for. "An anemone," Auggie says. "What are you looking for?"

"A water näcken," says Elias. In that moment, he looks like one—cross-legged on the boulder, poised to lure them with sweet music. He scrawls hurriedly in his notebook, like the poem is his urgent last. Now and then, he looks up to smile at Auggie, who smiles back. They share an expression, both wounded and pleased, that comes from paying too close attention to the world.

When she carries her son home, he is limp in her arms from so much wind and sun, his long legs dangling, his breath hot against her cheek.

She lays him down. "Sleep well."

He mumbles back, "In holy peace."

An echo of her old prayer, though she has not spoken it aloud in years. Still, he must have heard it somewhere. In church, perhaps, though she cannot be certain.

So often, she is mystified by him and how and where he gathers all he knows.

She sneaks out to Ulrika's cabin. Now, it belongs to Bea.

Alone there, she feels most herself, returned to herself, like cool water pouring into an empty vessel. She lines up her offerings: dead dragonfly, rattling poppy pod, hollow bone intricate as lace.

Crows fly in place against the wind. Snow falls in early October, flakes shimmery and fine stinging their cheeks. By November, the bay freezes clear to the mainland for the first time in seventy years. Over a forearm's length thick the fishermen say. No ferry, not much but sour herring and hard tack on the store shelves and the sun on its way to setting by noon. She pulls Auggie to the shore in the sled. The ocean is disguised as miles and miles of snow-covered field. Turkey tracks look like overlapping arrows, pointing in all directions. She glides him out to the edge of the harbor, where she lies down on her back and spreads her arms wide. Beside her, Auggie presses his face into the snow. This is how he makes his angels. He rises carefully, red-cheeked, from the impression of his eyes and nose and mouth. He is sad to leave their two forms behind.

The ice rises and falls with the gentle, persistent swell of the ocean beneath it. It would hold from shore to shore if she wanted to cross.

December, when the village girls process the church with candles, Auggie wants his own candle and crown. She sits beside August in the parlor draped with pine boughs to watch their son in his nightgown—curls wreathed in lingonberry—guard his candle flame and sing, "In our dark house she comes, bearing light."

January brings a world encased in ice. Every surface shines, blue tinged, the leaves left on the trees still as statuary. Boughs droop with new weight. All morning, the sound of gunshots as they snap from their trunks.

Come February, unusual warmth. Water courses from the gutters. Blocks of snow slide off the roof and land with bodily thuds. The bay thaws. The wind carries the unmistakable mulch scent of spring. False spring. Enough to trick crocuses into flowering before the next freeze.

In the bow of her father's old rowboat, Auggie holds tight to the picnic basket, compass around his neck. Bea remembers her father rowing for what seemed then like hours, the Blue Maiden over his shoulder no closer though he tugged hard on the oars, as if with each stroke the little island receded. Now, the current seems to carry them there.

Auggie darts from the boat and up the embankment, eager to explore without her, a strange companion she must once more get to know. How quickly her boy changes, each season ushering in a new iteration of his being.

"Please be careful," she calls.

She pulls her mother's stone from her pocket and places it at her feet. Right away, it is lost among the others.

On the bluff where Helmi was tied, she scans tree trunks for a rope long ago disintegrated.

"Come see," his distant voice carries. "A house. A labyrinth."

"Don't make up stories," she answers, and then, "Don't walk it." She follows the sound of him through gnarled wood and hanging moss to the spiraling path of stones laid on the ledge. "Mama," he calls faintly, from somewhere just out of sight. She shouts for him to come back. Their picnic is waiting.

She enters the labyrinth.

And she walks and she walks, in unexpected ease and low light. Who knows how much time passes. When she seems so close to finished, she is veered off to the outer ring. She continues. It comes as a surprise, to find herself at last at the center.

Acknowledgments

I must acknowledge the 65 women and 6 men executed in the Torsåker witch trials of 1674–1675. And I am indebted to Jöns Hornæus's account of that day "En Sannfärdig Berättelse" (A Truthful Story), as well as *The Malleus Maleficarum* by Heinrich Kramer, *Saducismus Triumphatus* by Joseph Glanvill, *Linnaeus's Öland and Gotland Journey 1741* translated by Marie Åsberg and William Stearn, "Sleuthing for Rare Plants on Fishers Island, Suffolk County, N.Y." by Edwin H. Horning, and *Svartkonstböcker: A Compendium of the Swedish Black Art Book Tradition* by Dr. Thomas K. Johnson, among many other sources indispensable to writing my fictional world.

Claudia Ballard, your advocacy is such a gift. Many thanks, also, to Camille Morgan and Oma Naraine.

Katie Raissian, to be your author is an honor and delight. Thank you for your warmth, patience, camaraderie, and unwavering guidance.

Elisabeth Schmitz, your support and feedback made all the difference. I'm so grateful to be in your excellent hands.

And to my exceptional team at Grove, especially Morgan Entrekin, John Mark Boling, Lilly Sandberg,

Gretchen Mergenthaler and Kelly Winton, and Laura Schmitt, for such kind attention.

To my communities of Putney, Beloit, the Iowa Writers' Workshop, and Fishers Island, your ongoing support means the world. Special thanks to Harry Bauld, Arran Bardige, Jade Daugherty, Chris Fink, Charles Baxter, Kevin Brockmeier, Lan Samantha Chang, Aurora Masum-Javed and Pierce Rafferty, extraordinary historian and neighbor. To the James Merrill House, Aspen Words, Yaddo, MacDowell, and with all my heart to Lighthouse Works, for creative connection and sustenance in so many forms. And to my early readers, for astounding insight and generosity: Jamie Watkins, Emma Törzs, Sara Martin, Jessie Gaynor, Liza Noyes (who I must thank twice) and the radiant Kiley McLaughlin.

Daily gratitude for Thomas Gebremedhin, brilliant mind and cherished friend. For Sean Hershey, beloved, who talked through my draft page by page. To my wonderful Malinowski and Noyes families, Karen, Wayne, ever-remarkable Uncle Terry, Mom, Bob, Kathleen, and my dear Dad, whose reverence for nature is woven into this book and my days. Thank you all, for loving me so well.

Finally, to my love Nate. You knew this book from the very start, as you see and know me. Your genius and sensitivity were key to its becoming in countless ways. Earliest reader, safest space, you support my work, as you do for so many, with absolute care. You make it all feel possible.

And always to Isla, a joy.